You wonder if he's the man of your dreams when:

- You propose at seven and it takes him fourteen years to make the next move.

- He dates cheerleaders when you aren't even close to being one.

- You see him in a suit and wish he was back in his sweats. Then you see him in his sweats and fantasize about him in his suit. Then you see him in your mother's kitchen and wish he was out on the porch. Then you see him on the porch and dream he's back in the kitchen. In other words, he's driving you nuts.

- Your brother won't let him date you, but your friends finally insist you must— for everyone's peace of mind.

Books by Janet Tronstad

Love Inspired

*An Angel for Dry Creek
*A Gentleman for Dry Creek
*A Bride for Dry Creek
*A Rich Man for Dry Creek
*A Hero for Dry Creek
*A Baby for Dry Creek
*A Dry Creek Christmas
*Sugar Plums for Dry Creek
*At Home in Dry Creek
**The Sisterhood of the Dropped Stitches
*A Match Made in Dry Creek
*Shepherds Abiding in Dry Creek
**A Dropped Stitches Christmas
*Dry Creek Sweethearts
**A Heart for the Dropped Stitches
*A Dry Creek Courtship
*Snowbound in Dry Creek
**A Dropped Stitches Wedding

*Dry Creek
**The Sisterhood of the Dropped Stitches

Love Inspired Historical

*Calico Christmas
  at Dry Creek

JANET TRONSTAD

Janet Tronstad grew up on a small farm in central Montana. One of her favorite things to do was to visit her grandfather's bookshelves, where he had a large collection of Zane Grey novels. She's always loved a good story. Today, Janet lives in Pasadena, California, where she is a full-time writer.

A Dropped Stitches Wedding
Janet Tronstad

Steeple Hill®

Published by Steeple Hill Books™

STEEPLE HILL BOOKS

Steeple Hill®

Recycling programs for this product may not exist in your area.

ISBN-13: 978-0-373-87522-1
ISBN-10:   0-373-87522-3

A DROPPED STITCHES WEDDING

Printed in U.S.A.

The Lord is my light and my salvation; whom shall I fear? The Lord is the strength of my life; of whom shall I be afraid?

—*Psalms* 27:1

This book is dedicated to a special lightbulb and the people who care for it. Except for two quick moves and a few power outages, this bulb has been burning continuously in a Livermore, California, fire station for over a hundred years. That's around-the-clock performance for more decades than most of us have been alive. The four-watt, carbon filament bulb was donated in 1901 by the owner of the Livermore Power and Light Company so firefighters wouldn't need to fumble around in the dark with kerosene lamps before going out to fight the night fires.

For the purposes of this book, I have taken the liberty of moving the lightbulb downstate from Livermore's Station No. 6 to a fictitious firehouse in Old Town Pasadena. The bulb's message remains undimmed, however. It serves as a reminder to all of us that when we care for things and make them last, we keep our world healthy and green.

My thanks to all of the California firefighters.
You do a great job.

Chapter One

"I am a typed director. If I made *Cinderella*, the audience would immediately be looking for a body in the coach."

—Alfred Hitchcock

Lightning flashed through the window when Marilee Davidson read this quote to us seven years ago. Earlier that evening she'd heard the thunder and written the words out on a piece of paper in her office down the hall from our meeting room. She smiled when she shared the quote with us, saying she just had to bring it—the night inspired thoughts of Hitchcock with every gust of the stormy wind.

Even back then, the Sisterhood of the Dropped Stitches started each meeting with a quote, and we loved this one. We could hardly knit at all that night, not with the thunder and then a discussion of perfectly ordinary things like shower curtains and birds that turned deadly. Hitchcock always could take something innocent and twist it around until shivers of fright raced down our spines. It was the first time in months that we talked about something besides cancer.

And then we realized our cancers were like a Hitchcock movie; all four of us had been caught unawares by them. One minute our bodies were perfectly ordinary teenage-girl ones, and the next minute—zap—they had turned against us. Just like those birds with their pointy beaks.

I had no sooner realized that fact than I took a smooth stone out of my pocket and began to rub it. Whenever I was nervous in those days, I'd rub my Lizzie stone. We all had things that comforted us back then. Marilee had those baseball caps she wore. Becca Snyder had her list of things to do (she was convinced she would get well if she just did everything she was supposed to do). Even Carly Winston had her flawless makeup; she believed that if she made herself look healthy, she would be healthy.

No wonder our counselor, Rose, had wanted us to meet together weekly. We might not have been able to speak all of our fears aloud, but we felt stronger simply by being together. In the end, it didn't matter if all we did was knit and brace ourselves against the next crash of thunder; we had each other.

I'm Lizabett MacDonald, and I refuse to shiver in the dark anymore, not even for Hitchcock. If I'm going to watch a movie, it's got to be a happy one.

It's Thursday evening and I'm walking down the street to meet the others for our weekly Sisterhood meeting. One thing Hitchcock knew was how to set the stage for momentous announcements, and I plan to make a big one tonight. I need to give my news some buildup, some atmosphere—some pizzazz. I can't just blurt everything out like it's nothing more than my order for a ginger-spiced caffe latte.

Right now, the sidewalks of Old Town Pasadena are dark except for the streetlamps and what little light shines out from the open stores. Fat drops of March rain are falling, and I see some distant lightning. I walk past the historic brick fire station, the upscale Italian restaurant and the gelato place with its fresh fruit toppings. I take careful steps and am carrying an umbrella, but my canvas shoes have become a little squishy.

I stop under the curved awning that hangs over the front door of the Pews diner. This is where I'm headed. I take a moment to listen, and I hear the rain beating down harder than I expected—still I'm sure I'll be able to hear a clap of thunder even if I'm inside the diner. And when I do hear the sound, I'll know it's my cue to tell everyone my plans. Very Hitchcockian.

I lower my umbrella and walk through the main part of the Pews until I reach the French doors that lead to the back room where the Sisterhood has met for years. My sweater and jeans are slightly damp from the rain, but I'm feeling good about myself.

I square my shoulders and throw open the doors. Everyone looks up, and I say hello. Nothing more. I'm going to wait for my signal before I make my announcement. I shake the raindrops off of my umbrella and walk over to the large oak table, where I pull out a chair and sit down with everyone else.

The others are knitting quietly, something that we do

at the beginning of every meeting. It's our thinking time. I lower my knitting bag to the floor and pull out some needles and yarn to begin work on the ivory afghan I'm making for my mother.

I feel like my news is almost bursting out of me. The sisters are going to be so excited. What's happening is that this coming Sunday—at church when the pastor asks if anyone wants to commit their life to Jesus—I'm going to stand right up. Which means I'll be saying *yes*. For me, this is an earth-shaking decision; I've been debating the whole thing for a few months. Finally, I decided to stop fretting and just go with what my heart tells me to do.

So, here I am waiting to announce my decision to my best friends.

The click of needles is all that I hear. I stop knitting for a minute. The air is moist from the rain, and I smell Uncle Lou's signature coffee brewing out front.

I'll be the last of the sisters to become a Christian, and I'm still a little new to the wonder of the whole idea. None of the others even know I've been meeting individually with the pastor, so they won't be expecting anything like this. After I tell them, the sisters will be stunned for a split second and then they'll explode with joy. Hugs and chaos are a given.

That's part of the reason why I want a ta-da moment before I tell everyone about it. I want to show that I realize it's a sacred moment and worthy of some ceremony. The other half of the reason is purely selfish; I get too chatty when I'm worried—or too silent. It's one or the other.

I have tried for years now to overcome my worried

state of mind. But I keep noticing that things never seem as likely to go bad as when my life is good, which means I'm constantly on edge—unless I'm utterly miserable. I know it sounds nuts. When people look at me, they see this bright smile plastered on my face, but inside my mind is waiting for the other shoe to drop. It seems there's always a payback for the good times—at least that's the way it happens in my life.

The sisters know I worry, but not many other people do. Even now, I try not to think about how scary-good everything is as I look around.

Marilee's Uncle Lou owns this diner, and he set this room aside for us years ago when he found out we were meeting in some depressing hospital room with nothing but nutrition charts on the walls. No one else uses this room, and we have a couple of shelves behind the table loaded with our books. Of course, the row of self-help psychology books is mine.

Initially, I wasn't in favor of meeting here because my big brother, Quinn, is one of those coffee-drinking firemen from the station down the street. I was afraid he'd be hanging around the Pews all of the time, and, being fifteen when we started meeting, I wanted my own place. Quinn promised not to darken the door here without an invitation, though, and over the years that we've been meeting here this place has become a sanctuary.

Tonight, the sisters are all here—Marilee, Carly, Becca and me. Our counselor, Rose, still comes sometimes, but she isn't here now. She spends most of her time with teenagers who have cancer, and since all of us have been free of the Big C for over seven years, she only comes to see us when *she* needs encouragement.

Which is kind of nice: that we can give her that after all she's done for us.

I stop for a moment. For the first time, I know who—besides Rose—to thank for the fact that we all came through our cancer just fine. *Thank you, Jesus.*

My quick gasp at that discovery must have been louder than I thought because Marilee looks at me, then glances at her watch and sets her knitting down on the table. That means our fifteen minutes of silent knitting are over. We usually continue to knit, but we chat while we're doing it.

"So, what's up?" Marilee turns to me and asks. She has this expectant look on her face like she knows I've got something to say. She's the earth mother in our group, and she notices things like who's on edge and has something to share. She's the one who holds us all together when anyone gets upset or has a problem.

Marilee is beautiful inside and out. I like the way her short brown hair settles around her face these days. Those baseball caps she used to wear pushed her hair down and made it hard to see her eyes. Of course, the caps were as comforting to her as my Lizzie stone is to me, so I'm glad she still has them hanging on pegs in her office down the hall from here. She's done the diner's bookkeeping for years.

"Is something wrong?" Marilee asks, looking at me with sympathy in her eyes. "Or is it just the nervous thing?"

I don't know how Marilee knows. I try not to say anything when I'm worried, but it must seep out my pores. None of the other sisters look surprised at her question, which probably means it's obvious to all of them, too.

I shake my head. "Don't worry. It's good news—really good news—but I'll save it for later."

I put my needles down and reach into my knitting bag to pull out a dozen fabric swatches. "Right now, we need to look at these. What do you think?"

I'm not the only one with good news. Tonight we are going to pick out the fabric for our bridesmaid dresses for Marilee's wedding, because—wonder of wonders—she is getting married to my dear brother, Quinn. They have already put in for their marriage license.

I can hardly contain myself. They told us all about it last month, and happiness bubbles up inside of me every time I think of them getting married. Which, of course, makes me half-afraid something is going to happen to ruin everything.

I try to keep these particular fears to myself, though. Quinn is so happy, and Marilee is—well, she looks at my brother with so much love in her eyes that I practically weep when I see it. They have both waited so long to find their own true love.

It reminds me of that idyllic summer I enjoyed before I found out about my cancer. I was floating along in a life that could have been an ad for one of those springtime soaps with all of the birds singing and the flowers blooming. And then wham—everything took a Hitchcockian twist so fast I couldn't quite grasp what was happening. My balmy summer was hit with nightmare storms. The flowers sprouted thorns. The birds sharpened their beaks. And something started destroying the muscles in my leg so fast I couldn't outrun it.

I hate to say it, but I know things could go that way for Marilee and Quinn, too. I try to push all of the nervous thoughts away, though. I don't want Marilee to see what's on my mind.

Instead, I focus on the good parts of the wedding.

I know just what Marilee wants on her day, too.

All four of us remember the long discussions we had about our dream weddings when we first battled cancer. Back then, Marilee always wore boy-cut jeans with men's flannel shirts and those baseball caps of hers. Underneath all of the tomboy stuff, though, she dreamed of having a wedding with a horse-drawn carriage and a princess dress that shimmered in the light of a thousand candles.

In one version, I think she was even wearing a tiara. Her cake was always a white confection that stood three feet tall and was served on little crystal plates while a full orchestra played in the background. Marilee used to get a dreamy expression in her eyes when she talked about her wedding back then. She even had a recipe for a special icing that gave the cake that lacy bridal look.

Of course, in the here and now, she's made a point of saying she doesn't really expect that kind of extravagance. She's resigned to reality. But that's not going to stop me. She doesn't know it, but I'm going to do everything I can to give her the fantasy wedding she used to talk about. After all, Cinderella didn't think she could go to the prince's ball, either, and she ended up there.

I should mention that Marilee and Quinn asked me to be their wedding planner. Only a youngest child can understand how big this is. It took years for Quinn to trust me to cross the street by myself. Now he's letting me plan his wedding to Marilee. It's one of the most significant days of his life, and I'll be in charge. I wonder if he's realized that yet.

I started my wedding crusade last week by emphatically vetoing Quinn's suggestion that they get married in the pastor's study. Hopefully, Quinn was joking, but I'm not sure. He backpedaled on his suggestion too soon for me to know if he was serious. I know Marilee wants to get married soon, too, but even she looked a little taken aback at the thought of an office.

"This looks nice," Marilee says as she picks up the sample swatch of shell-pink satin that I just put on the table. "It might be too cotton-candy sweet, though."

Needless to say, I want everything to be as close to perfect as possible. I want the right dress. The right cake. The right music. The right carriage (they do have a horse and buggy in Pasadena that I can rent). I owe Quinn and Marilee both so much for their support of me that I am hoping I can repay some of it by surprising them with the ultimate dream wedding.

Cash is scarce now that Quinn is making those mortgage payments on his condo. He earns good money as a fireman, but he says they need furniture more than they need an elegant wedding. I disagree with him, of course. They're only going to have one wedding, and they'll probably have a dozen sofas during their life together.

But Quinn is a practical kind of guy, so I promised we'd find a way to do the wedding without spending too much money. I didn't tell him, but the hospitality courses I am taking at Pasadena City College have taught me a lot about wedding plans. We students get all kinds of bridal promotions, like discount coupons and even some free things. I should be able to do a fantasy wedding on a modest wedding budget. Besides, parts of the fantasy don't require money. Like getting the right colors.

Light pink is the color Marilee mentioned the most years ago when we sat around sharing our dreams. So I spent hours this afternoon walking through the garment district downtown. I got a blister on my left foot, but I also managed to find a dozen different shades of pink fabric. I don't know if Marilee will want shell pink or coral pink or maybe just a blush, so I brought sample clips of fabric in all those colors and more with me.

"It's supposed to be sweet," I say in answer to Marilee's question as I finger the smooth silk of the coral pink. "It's your wedding. You should pick whatever color you want."

The rain is really coming down now, and I wonder if I should go over and close the window. It's only opened slightly and there's an awning over it. No rain is coming inside, so I stay where I am.

"Absolutely. Whatever you want," Becca agrees. She's counting stitches in the scarf she's knitting, and I can tell by the look on her face that she's not really listening.

"I just can't see you in pink," Marilee says with a frown in Becca's direction.

Well, that makes Becca look up. It clearly hasn't occurred to her until right now that *she* will be wearing one of the bridesmaid dresses, too. Becca opens her mouth and then closes it just as quick.

Those courses I took warned me this could happen. A bride often wavers in what she really wants (or is bent by the pressure of family and friends), and it's the job of the wedding planner to keep the bride focused on her true vision. A happy bride makes a joyous wedding, which sets a foundation for a good marriage and a peaceful life together. So even colors can be important.

"You always said it's how you pictured things," I remind everyone before Becca can say anything. I know the other sisters are thinking about those old wedding dreams we shared. We all had our preferences. Becca, for instance, wanted her bridesmaids to wear black. I suspect she's outgrown that decision by now. I look over at her. On second thought, maybe not. Judging by the expression on her face, she might still rather go with black than any of the colors I have in my hand. But she swallows bravely.

"I can wear pink," Becca says with some grit in her voice. "Don't worry about me."

Good for Becca.

Becca's in law school, and she looks like an attorney no matter what she wears. Her dark brown hair is long and she twists it up in a knot on the back of her head. She has an olive complexion and doesn't need any makeup on her delicate features. I sometimes think it's the intensity in her eyes that makes her look so much like a lawyer. I've got to say, though, that pink really isn't her color.

Carly is the one in our group who will look the best in pink. She's already as rosy and white as a Dresden figurine. And she was the Rose Queen in the annual New Year's parade before she got her cancer diagnosis. Now she's a student like me, and she works as a waitress in the diner here to pay her way. But she still has that San Marino rich-girl look even if she doesn't actually have the money we always thought she had to go with it.

Last year, after Carly moved out of her uncle's house and let her hair go back to its natural brown color, she added blond highlights to make it look even more stylish. She'd look perfect in any of the pink shades we have. I expect her to get discovered by a casting agent one day soon and be filmed gliding down some sweeping staircase like they have in *Gone with the Wind*.

"I don't know," Marilee says with a small frown as she looks at us all. She's fingering the pink fabric samples.

"I do have others," I say as I spread the rest of the swatches around. They're all different colors. A wedding planner should always be prepared with alternatives. I even have a fire-engine red in case they want to do something honoring Quinn's job. The guys from the fire station down the street come into the Pews often after their shifts. I've even relented and told Quinn he can come sometimes.

"The men have it easy," Marilee says as she flips through the new swatches. "They all know they're wearing a standard tuxedo. Quinn just wants the black and white ones."

"Men always look good in tuxedoes," I agree. I remind myself to get some information from tuxedo rental places. I'll need that for the wedding-planner kit that I'm putting together. If all goes well with this wedding, I plan to set myself up in business. Therefore, I'm going to take photos at the various stages of planning to use in my brochure.

"I just can't believe I'm getting married," Marilee says as she lays down the fabric swatches and leans back in her chair. She glances over at me. "I always thought you would be the first one to walk down the aisle."

"Me?" I blink. *Me?* I look at her. "I'm the youngest—I never do anything first."

Seriously. I was the last one to get my all-clear from cancer. The last one to graduate from high school. The last one to decide to get right with God. The last one to be trusted with anything like planning a wedding. Even the last one here tonight.

"Believe me, I'll be the last one of us to get married."

"I don't know why. You've had your groom picked out since you were in grade school," Marilee says. "That's more than the rest of us had going for us at that age."

This, of course, makes the others look at me with interest. We'd all rather talk about men than knit any day, even if we've already had this particular discussion a few times before.

"I was just a kid. What did I know? Those days are long gone." I stand up and walk over to pull the window down.

"When you've had a crush on a guy for that long, he only gets more intriguing with time," Becca says. I turn around and see a gleam in her eyes that makes me uneasy. Becca's always telling us that we need to take more risks in life. She continues like I knew she would, "You should just go ahead and ask him out. What do you have to lose?"

I wonder if she's getting back at me for all of those pink samples. *What do I have to lose? My self-respect, for one thing. My sanity, for another. Maybe even my heart if I'm not careful.*

I walk back and sit down. "I wouldn't ask Rick Kiefer out if he were the last man on earth. You know that."

Together with my brother, Rick ruled my childhood. He grew up in the house next to us, and he has worked at the same fire station as my brother for years now. To my everlasting mortification, I proposed to Rick when I was too young to know better, and the memory still haunts me.

Becca nods. "Well, if he were the last man on earth, he'd be in demand. But he's not—there's no line of women in his life. He can't have more than—what— twenty girlfriends about right now?"

"He certainly doesn't have twenty girlfriends. He'd never—" I stop. Becca is grinning at me. "Okay, so maybe he's not the *worst* man in the world. He wouldn't cheat on his wife. Ever."

He wouldn't hesitate to break a little girl's heart, though, I think to myself indignantly. I was only seven. He could have suggested a long engagement or something. What did I know about getting married? I probably just wanted the cake.

"Well, that's important," Carly says. "You don't want a husband who will cheat on you."

Rick's parents are divorced, and cheating played a part in it. He might break a woman's heart, but he wouldn't betray her. And, of course, he does go into burning buildings to save people's lives. He's not a bad person even if he is totally blind to me as a woman.

Carly adds, "Isn't he the one who gave you that little rock you carry around? I always thought that was kind of sweet."

"That happened a million years ago," I mumble. She knows very well Rick gave me the Lizzie stone. She just wants to remind me that he did.

I can remember it without her nudging, though. It

was my first day of kindergarten and I was almost in tears before I even got to school. I was walking with Rick, and he reached into his pocket and pulled out a stone. He told me it was a Lizzie stone, named for me, and if things were bad, all I had to do was rub the stone and everything would be better. I was only five, and he hadn't broken my heart yet, so I believed him completely.

Later, of course, I realized he'd probably just picked the rock up to throw at a tree for target practice. It wasn't even a pretty rock, just a dull, weathered gray stone that might have sat next to the sidewalk for decades.

In his defense, I'm sure Rick hadn't known what in the world to do with me when I started to cry; we hadn't gotten to the school grounds yet, so there was no adult he could hand me off to. And I know he felt sorry for me. My life had been in a tailspin back then. My father had died that summer and all I wanted to do was stay home and curl up in my blanket. But my mother said we all needed to be brave, and that meant I had to go to school as planned.

For some reason, no one in my family could walk with me that first day, so Rick had reluctantly agreed to do it. He was the only neighborhood kid brave enough to keep coming over to our house during those funeral days.

Still, it wasn't right.

"He was taking advantage of my fears to make himself look like a hero," I say, wondering if my tendency to worry started that day with Rick. He had no business giving me false hope; it made me feel like I could do something to change my crumbling world.

I really believed back then that if I only rubbed that

stone hard enough, everything in my life would be right again. It was a lot of responsibility, and I took it seriously. Nowadays, rubbing the Lizzie stone is just habit, but it wasn't that way back then. I thought it had power because Rick said it did. If he had told me it would change grass into green cheese, I would have believed him. If the stone wasn't working, it had to be my fault.

No wonder I expected, when I proposed two years later, that he'd accept. He had led me to think the Lizzie stone could give me all my heart desired.

Marilee shrugs. "He couldn't have been very old."

"Nine," I say.

He wasn't much older when he refused my offer of marriage. Well, it wasn't so much a refusal as it was a moment of shocked disbelief—followed by a burst of laughter so loud and so long I finally kicked him in the shins and told him no one would ever marry him if he was such a horrible, terrible boy. That only made him fall down and roll on the ground, clutching his sides, until I was sure someone would look out their window and come running to see if he was having a fit like the dog down the street had that one time.

I pause a minute to let it sink in to everyone that the man and I have way too much history to date. Besides...

"In the eyes of Rick Kiefer, I will always just be Quinn's little sister," I add softly. "It would never work."

And that is the bottom line. I have spent my whole life being the last and the youngest in everything. I have no intention of marrying someone who will treat me like a little sister. Even without the sister part, I want to be treated like a responsible adult by my husband. I try to think of the words to say what I mean without making any of the sisters feel like they have babied me—mostly because sometimes they did when we were sick—but I hesitate, and Marilee starts eyeing me with speculation.

"Quinn tells me Rick isn't dating anyone at the moment," she finally says. "He hasn't even asked anyone out for a while. Almost a year—"

"You didn't say anything about Rick, did you?" I hold my breath. It never occurred to me until now that Marilee knows everything and that, since she's obviously grown closer to Quinn, my secrets might be spilling over. I don't want Quinn to know how I used to feel about his best friend. At least I've been spared that humiliation.

"I only asked if Rick would want to bring a guest to the wedding," Marilee says. "Quinn doesn't have any idea that you're interested in his best man."

"That's good, because I'm *not* interested. I haven't been for years." I reach down into the pocket of my sweater and start rubbing that stone again. It might not have any power, but it does soothe my nerves.

"I suppose it's just as well," Marilee adds with a twinkle in her eyes. "Quinn would tell Rick to stay away from you anyway if he thought you were inclined in that direction."

She's got that right. When it comes to being overprotective about guys, my brother is the worst. In high school, he didn't agree to let me date anyone, not even the math geeks. He certainly wouldn't have let me date a heartbreaker like Rick. Not that it was ever an issue. Rick was four years older than me and too busy dating the cheerleaders to notice me. And I went out with a couple of the math geeks anyway.

"I still say you should ask Rick out," Becca says. "How's the man supposed to know you're interested?"

"I'm *not* interested," I say. Doesn't anyone ever listen? "Besides, it's not like we never talk. I see him practically every week when he's hanging around with Quinn. If Rick wanted to ask me out, he would."

I'd say no if he did ask me, of course, but Rick has a dozen different ways to convince a woman to go out with him. He once asked out a woman in a department store while he was buying socks. *Socks!* And they were just those cheap white ones. He got her to say yes, too.

"How's he supposed to ask you out if the only time he sees you Quinn is around?" Becca asks. "That's too big-brother's-watching for anyone."

"Rick doesn't want to ask me out," I repeat patiently. "So it doesn't matter who else is there."

Even if he never sees me alone, Rick sees me often enough to ask any question he has on his mind. I had to move back to my mom's house while I finish up my classes at the city college. And even though Quinn has a townhouse in Altadena, he's at Mom's a lot, especially around mealtimes. Half of the time, Rick is with him. Mom loves it, of course. She adopted Rick as an honorary son years ago when his mother ran off to find herself by painting watercolors in Laguna Beach.

"It's not always easy for guys to ask a woman out," Carly offers gently.

I know it may not be easy for guys to ask out beauty queens like Carly, but ordinary women like me don't have that same effect on men.

"I thought maybe Rick had already asked you out," Marilee adds calmly.

"What?" *Whatever gave her that idea?* I look at her in astonishment.

"Your news," Marilee reminds me. "You mentioned you had news, and I thought that might be it."

I shake my head. Just then a clap of thunder sounds. It is what I have been waiting for, but I can't make my announcement now. For one thing, I'm speechless. Marilee thought Rick had asked me out? What would have given her that idea?

"I wonder why he asked what kind of restaurants you like, then?" Marilee asks, almost like she's talking to herself. "It seemed important to him."

My ears are hearing the kind of squeals I had expected, but the news is all wrong.

"Rick knows where I like to eat," I manage to say. "For one thing, I come here every chance I get. That's no big secret."

"But he wouldn't bring you to the Pews on a date," Carly protests. "Half of the fire department is out front some nights. He'd want someplace private, you know—romantic with candlelight."

"Maybe with some music, too. You like music," Becca adds. "Oh, I wonder if there's a place that plays ballet music. You'd love that."

"Trust me. Rick Kiefer is *not* asking me out," I say with a little more force than is strictly necessary. "And I doubt he even knows what ballet music sounds like. He's known me for years, and he's never asked me out."

Actually, he's never even come to the Pews to eat with his buddies. I've always wondered if it was because I'm here so much. Maybe he doesn't want anyone to see him talking with me. How lowering is that?

"Maybe he suddenly realized you've grown up," Becca says. "It happens."

"I look the same as I have for years," I counter.

When I say it out loud like that, it doesn't sound so good. I can see the same thought is occurring to the others as well.

"Maybe a new hairstyle would be nice," Becca says.

"And some of that new eye makeup," Carly adds. "I've got just the thing."

Before I know it, I'm booked for a haircut and a makeover on Saturday afternoon. It would be happening tomorrow except I have classes. Once the talk moved to mascara and hair tints, I couldn't think of any way to bring the flow of chatter back to the news I did want to share. I wonder if Hitchcock ever ran into a problem like this, where his scenes took on a life of their own and he couldn't keep them under control.

Oh, well, I will see the sisters again on Saturday for my makeover. They insist they want to lend moral support at the cosmetic counter in Macy's. My news can wait until after we finish there. It doesn't seem right to bring up my eternal soul when they're all worried about what kind of eyeliner I should wear.

I wonder if God cares about my eyeliner. Or me and Rick.

I do a reality check. There is no me and Rick. There's no chance he is going to ask me out. And it's a good thing. If he did ask me for a date, I probably wouldn't live through the worry of it.

I reach into my pocket for the Lizzie stone and start to rub my thumb over its surface. Just imagine how much bad could happen if, through some strange Hitchcockian twist in the universe, my dream date did come true just like I had always pictured it would. The intimate talking with our heads close together, the searing kiss on the lips—those two wonderful things could bring a terrifying backlash, sort of like those sweet birds that morphed into sharp-beaked killers for Hitchcock.

No, I tell myself firmly, it's really for the best that Rick never asks me out.

Chapter Two

"He obliged Cinderella to sit down, and, putting the slipper to her little foot, he found it went on very easily, and fitted her as if it had been made of wax."

—Charles Perrault in "Cinderella"

After we had the Hitchcock quote, I decided to balance things out, and I brought one of my favorites from Cinderella. I was in the middle of chemo, and I wore slippers more often than I wore my regular shoes. I joked that we all had something in common with the prince's favorite lady—our feet were made for slippers.

Rose started knitting us slippers that night in rainbow colors. Mine were fuchsia. Marilee's turquoise. Carly's emerald. And Becca's bright yellow. I still have those slippers.

Morning light spills into the upstairs room in my mother's house. This is the bedroom where I spent my childhood and my sick years. The room always feels jumbled to me; I have too many things left over from the days when I was growing up.

Usually, I'm a little annoyed with the clutter, but this morning I'm not. I see those fuchsia slippers sitting under my old stuffed animals and I go put them on my feet. I can climb mountains in these slippers. Figuratively, of course. I used them when I pretended to be a ballerina during my time with cancer. Despite everything, I clung to the belief that I could someday be a real ballerina. Every chance I had, I glided across this floor as best as I could in those slippers. Because I had a tendency to stumble, I could only do this when no one else was home. Both Quinn and my mother scolded me when they saw me try my ballet moves.

I must be remembering all of this because of the conversation with the sisters last night. By now I've realized, of course, that a date between Rick and me will never happen. And it's okay. It's also too bad. Rick grew out of his insensitive stage. I've never told the sisters, but I won't ever forget the time he caught me trying to glide across the living room floor in these slippers shortly after cancer had taken hold in my leg. He must have been eighteen or nineteen then.

Rick had come by looking for Quinn—who was gone, of course, or I wouldn't have been trying to do my ballet moves. I don't know how long Rick watched me through the locked screen door before he said my name. I thought he would scold me, too—or worse, laugh at me. But instead he asked if he could help. Because of my leg, I was having trouble actually gliding anywhere. But with Rick's arms supporting me, I swirled around that living room floor almost like I did in my dreams.

I knew Rick was doing it because of the cancer and all, but I lived for months on the memory of being able to move like that. He never said anything to anyone about it, either. I'm sure he forgot about it as soon as it was over, but I never will.

I take a twirl in my slippers just to remind myself that I am now able to make ballet moves all on my own, and then I go sit down on my bed.

I had left the Sisterhood journal on the nightstand beside me last night. Each of the sisters has already taken their turn with the journal, and the pages are bursting with life. Some pages have been stapled together. Others were bent back for a time, but are now open for everyone to read. The other sisters wrote down their hearts in this journal, each when it was her turn. And sometimes, when a sister wasn't ready for the others to read what she'd written, she fastened the pages shut.

Marilee is the one who started us with the journal. We each had different cancers—Marilee with her breast cancer, Carly with Hodgkin's disease, Becca with her bone tumor and me with it in the muscle of my leg. But our experience was the same, and Marilee believes that the story of how we reclaimed our lives after cancer will be helpful to others who currently have the disease.

I think Marilee is right, but the journal is becoming about more than our cancer days. The journal itself is helping us to pull our lives back together in the here and now. It's the place where we speak our fears and our joys. We missed so much in the years when we were sick; we need to make up for some of it now.

I wrote in the journal before I went to sleep last night, trying to describe my decision to become a Christian. I pick it up now to read what I wrote.

I feel like I'm one of those chicken-and-egg puzzles. What came first? God pulling me to Him or me getting curious about Him? Or did it all happen at the same time?

I have so many questions. I see the very first signs of what my life as a Christian will be like, and, frankly, it feels like I'm starting to tug on a thread. I wonder if everything that has gone before will unravel as I keep pulling that thread. Maybe God really is a knitter like Marilee used to say.

When God says He can make something new out of me, what does He really mean? Will He unravel me like a sweater? And what does He do with the stuff He takes out of me when He makes me new? Maybe He does fix His dropped stitches—Marilee always said our cancers were like careless stitches God had dropped when He was making us. I used to think I was the one who made the mistakes somehow. Or was it just the way life goes? Or is there some purpose to things that look like mistakes?

I have so many questions. But my main one is this—will God stop everything bad from happening in my life once I'm His? If that's true, maybe I can stop looking at the good times as a warning of bad things to come. Maybe the sisters won't need to worry about me anymore—

* * *

That's the end of what I wrote. Those are only the first of the words, though. I plan to continue describing the feelings inside of me as they happen in case Marilee is right and someone reads these words. They might be curious about what it feels like step-by-step to become a Christian. I know I used to wonder if there were any strange sensations when the other sisters became Christians. It didn't seem right to ask them, though, so I kept quiet. But I'm sure others have similar questions.

So I'm planning to write it all down in as much detail as possible so everyone will know—like those people who document their diseases. I plan to talk about everything that happens as I walk up that aisle. Like, will a warm electric sizzle race through my bones? Or will a light sensation flood my head, sort of a giddy thing? Will I be released of every worry I've ever had? Whatever I feel, I plan to put it down in black and white in a scientific manner. I hope it's nothing too strange.

In the meantime, the smell of coffee has started to tempt me to go downstairs. I pull on a pair of sweatpants and a T-shirt and run a brush through my hair. Quinn has seen me looking worse, and I hear his voice so I'm assuming he's down there talking to Mom while he's making one of his breakfasts. I'm glad that, even with his condo in Altadena, he comes by Mom's place a lot. He loves to cook breakfast, and I'm generally in favor of that since he's pretty good at it.

I'm still half-asleep, but I wake up quick enough when I step into the kitchen and see that my mother is nowhere around. And Quinn has company.

"Oh," I squeak and turn to go back up the stairs.

It's too late, though.

"It's just Rick," Quinn says. The two men are sitting at the table with mugs of coffee in front of them. "I'm going to make French toast in a minute."

"Hey, Lizzie," Rick says as he nods at me. He's the only one who calls me that, and he knows I hate it. He started calling me that after he gave me my Lizzie stone. I suppose he felt he had the right when he'd seen me at my kindergarten worst.

"What brings you here today?" I ask as politely as I can.

I notice Rick doesn't seem alarmed that I look like a disaster, which isn't good news. In fact, he has the same tolerant expression on his face that Quinn does. I'm glad the other sisters can't see this. They'd demand my makeover be even more extreme than they already plan. No one wants Rick to see me through a brother's eyes.

"Breakfast," Rick says, and then he gives me enough of a grin that I realize he's very aware of how I look and he's enjoying my discomfort.

"I forgot something," I say as I head back up the stairs.

Two minutes later, I'm standing in front of the mirror. I've changed my sweats for a pair of jeans and my T-shirt for a little pink sweater. I can't decide what to put on my lips so I settle for a pink gloss.

I put on silver earrings and slip a chunky pink ring on my finger. I've always gone for the pixie look, mostly because it's a natural one for me. My features are small and my auburn hair curls with abandon, so I have to spritz it a little to make it fall into some semblance of order. I swish some mascara on my eyelashes so I look as sultry as I can at this hour of the day.

At the last minute, I decide to leave my slippers on.

When I walk into the kitchen the second time, I try to move with the grace I acquired in all of those ballet classes I eventually took after my cancer.

"Sleep okay?" Quinn says from where he now stands by the stove. He's got a griddle on the burner and some sliced bread nearby. He turns and gives me a funny look.

I nod. "I always sleep good after our Sisterhood meetings."

He's probably wondering why I went upstairs and changed my clothes, but I'm not going to answer that question. Let him think I tore a seam in my sweatpants.

"Was everyone there?" my brother asks as he turns back to the skillet. He picks up a slice of bread and dips it into the bowl that must contain the egg mixture.

"Except for Rose," I say as I hear the sizzle of the bread hitting the skillet. Quinn makes his French toast a little crispy, and I like it. With some butter and maple syrup, it's heavenly.

Rick grunts at this, and I look over to where he's still sitting at the table. He's got the sleeves on his gray sweatshirt pushed up to his elbows. I think he's been out jogging already.

"What do you guys talk about at those meetings anyway?" he asks.

I pull up a chair and sit down at the table opposite the man. The morning sun shines in and covers us both. My mother's kitchen table has been in this same sunny spot for over thirty years. It's got a butcher-block top and a cluster of stuff in the center—a couple of salt and pepper shakers, a holder for paper napkins, a bowl for sugar and a few stray postage stamps. As humble as the whole setting is, it's one of my favorite places in the world.

"We talk about regular stuff," I say.

I'm sitting right across the table from Rick, and he keeps looking at me. I wonder if he suspects we sometimes talk about him in our Sisterhood meetings. Fortunately, I trust Marilee enough to know she'd never tell Quinn something like that. And if Quinn doesn't know, Rick can't possibly know.

"We knit, too," I add brightly.

"Yeah, that dropped stitch stuff," he says.

Rick has a classic chin with just a hint of dark whiskers. His thick black hair is longish. His eyes change from golden to brown whenever emotions rush through him. Usually, laughter keeps them light. The funny thing is that I didn't notice his looks for years. He was just Rick to me. He might have hung the stars in the sky for me when I was seven, but I didn't notice how drop-dead gorgeous he is until recently.

Just then Quinn brings a platter of French toast over to the table.

"I'll get some plates," I say as I stand.

"None for me," Quinn says, his voice sounding strained. "I need to, ah—make a phone call first. You two go ahead, though."

"Don't be silly," I say as I reach for the plates in the cupboard. "We can wait for you to make a phone call."

I pull the plates out of the cupboard and open the drawer to get forks.

"The call will take some time," Quinn says as he starts to walk to the door leading to the living room. He sounds almost guilty about something. "You don't want the French toast to get cold."

"Oh," I say as I put the plates and forks on the table.

I sit down and look over at Rick. "What's with him?"

Something is going on. Rick has an odd look on his face, too.

"Did Quinn put cayenne pepper on the French toast?" I ask. He did that once years ago. He thought it was funny to watch me take a bite. I would think he would have better sense than to do that now, though, especially because I'm his wedding planner.

Rick grins. "No pepper that I know of."

"Then what's with him?" I can't think of any phone call that needs to be made that quickly. "It only takes him five minutes to eat."

I pull one of the plates toward me. I rather ungraciously push the other one in Rick's direction. Then I spear some French toast with my fork.

"And he knows the toast is no good when it's cold. You'd think—" I stop. The food falls unnoticed to my plate, and I rest my hand on the table. "Quinn's not calling a doctor, is he? Did he have some tests? Is he sick?"

The fear rolls in fast. That's one thing we share in the Sisterhood. We all realize how swiftly those we love can become seriously ill. Quinn looks okay, but—

"No." Rick reaches out his hand as though he knows what I'm thinking. He stops before he pats my hand, however, and pulls back. "Quinn is just trying to give us some privacy."

"Us?" I notice Rick is not looking me in the eye.

Now that I'm not worried about my brother, I'm starting to be a little annoyed with him. This is worse than the pepper.

"Yeah, so we can talk," Rick says slowly. Now he looks at me like I should understand everything he's saying.

"Okay—" Maybe I am slow, because I sure can't figure this out.

"I know you're spending a lot of time with this wedding business," Rick continues.

"It's not wedding *business*. It's the most glorious day in a couple's life together," I say. At least, that much I know. "Two people are proclaiming their love for each other for the whole world to see. It's the ultimate in commitment. And romance."

"Yeah, well—"

Rick is back to looking uncomfortable. Suddenly, I figure it out.

"Quinn asked you to get me to agree to have their wedding in the pastor's study, didn't he? I knew he wouldn't let that go. But it's not a good idea. You can tell him that. Marilee wants flowers and friends around and the blessing of the whole church. She deserves all of that. They're only going to get married once—they should make it memorable."

I stand up in protest and then reach down and grab my plate with the French toast on it. I figure I can go outside and eat on the porch. There's no need for me to miss out on a perfectly fine breakfast just because my brother is clueless when it comes to his wedding. Not that his best friend is any more enlightened.

"No, no—that's not what I'm doing," Rick says. "Really, I think they should have any kind of wedding they want."

"Really?" I ask a little skeptically.

Rick nods.

"I suppose it's the tuxedos then." I set my plate back and sit down on the chair. "Guys never like to wear them. You'd think they were straitjackets the way they complain about the tie and that cumberbund thing. They should try wearing a bridesmaid's dress if they want someone to feel sorry for them."

"I don't care about ties," Rick says as he runs his fingers through his hair. "Would you just listen to me— I'm not worried about Quinn's wedding. He can get married anywhere he wants, wearing anything he wants. What I'm trying to do is ask you to have dinner with me tomorrow night."

Okay, now I feel a little foolish. "Dinner?"

"Yeah, you know, the evening meal. It's a custom. People eating together."

"I don't—"

I'm trying to remember what I decided to say if Rick ever asked me out. I used to fantasize about this conversation a lot in my younger years. So much time has passed, though, that I forgot all the clever things I was going to say. Whoever thought he would wait this many years to make a move?

"I could use your advice," he finally adds. "I'm in charge of the One Hundred and Five party for the light-bulb down at the station, and I could use some pointers. It's only a couple of weeks away."

I know that sounds strange. But the lightbulb is a big deal around here. And I did hear that Rick has been in charge of it for a while. Not that I figured there was a whole lot to do. The bulb has been burning steadily all those years now without help from anyone. Of course, people are amazed that it's still going. It's been written up by *Ripley's Believe It or Not!* and the *Los Angeles Times*.

The bulb was screwed into a beam of the old firehouse on Colorado Boulevard in the early 1900s so that the firemen back then wouldn't need to light kerosene lanterns before they pulled on their gear and went out to fight the night fires. No one ever turns the thing off, and it just keeps lighting up the night.

"I wish the department wouldn't do these five-year things," Rick says as he runs his hands through his hair. "At least for the hundred-year ceremony, they hired someone outside the department to coordinate everything."

"Well, this one doesn't need to be as formal as that ceremony," I say. "Isn't this just a local thing?"

"Oh, there's still bound to be rules," Rick says. "And I keep thinking I'll get something backward. The wrong people will be invited or someone will decide to touch the lightbulb and break it. Nobody is even allowed to dust it down at the station. But with strangers around, we need to be careful. And if some fool breaks it, I'll be responsible because I didn't have the signs hanging in the right places or a guard posted or something."

"I don't know much about hanging signs," I mumble and then realize, "Besides, isn't that bulb up high? No one could get up there unless they had a ladder."

He waves my protest away. "We're a fire station; we practically invented the ladder. I wouldn't be able to face the other guys if something goes wrong. Someone breaking the thing was just an example. A million other things could happen."

He's right, of course. A million and one things can happen in any public event. We learned that in the hospitality courses I've been taking. And I know this isn't some ordinary ceremony for Rick.

Quinn has told me that the firemen joke that if any of them mistakenly break that lightbulb, they'll have to leave the department. They might even need to leave the state if they want to keep a job as a fireman. Not every fire station has a mascot, but this one does—and they protect it as only firemen can.

"Please," Rick adds. "I could use the help."

I look at him skeptically. I've never known Rick to be a worrier. But I can see why this lightbulb would be a big thing to him. And he doesn't usually plan events that have press coverage. At least I think—

"Is the *Star News* covering it?" I ask.

Rick shrugs. "They have in the past, but this year I don't know. The hundred-year mark was the big event. I keep trying to think of something to jazz everything up. Things just won't be the same with no media there. And it *is* a big event this year because no one knows about the future of the fire station. There's talk of retiring it as an active station—it's been half-retired anyway since they built the new place next door. More and more of the action happens there. Before long, they might even tear the old one down. "

"Oh dear." That is a big thing.

"So the station *needs* this event to go well." Rick says. "The captain says maybe we need to start renting the old building out for kid's birthday parties. He's sort of joking, but we need to think of something to make the place useful."

Then he sighs. Rick knows very well that I can't ignore someone who is that worried and for good cause.

That fire station is a landmark; surely no one would tear it down. Would they? Actually, someone might. The city would make lots of money if they sold it.

"I suppose I can review your plans with you," I say. "Just to give you an objective opinion on things."

"Great," Rick says. All of a sudden, he doesn't seem concerned about anything. "Would seven o'clock be a good time to pick you up?"

I nod as I lift up my fork. "But tell Quinn he doesn't need to leave the room for you to ask me for help with something like that. He must already know you're planning the—what do you call it anyway?"

I cut into my French toast.

"We call it the One Hundred and Five Celebration," Rick says. "We had a contest to come up with the name."

If they had a contest and came up with that for a name, they really do need some help to make this a memorable event. I would feel terrible if something happened to that fire station and I could have done something to save it.

"Well, try not to worry," I say. "The guys you work with are a great group. They'll understand if you can't pull in enough publicity to save the station."

"Yeah, well," Rick mutters like he's none too happy, "I guess it wouldn't be so bad getting a different job. Work won't be like it used to be anyway with everyone getting married."

Suddenly I get it. I set my fork down and reach across the table to put my hand over his.

"I know it's hard when your best friend gets married," I say, feeling sympathy now that I understand what's bothering him. "But I know my brother. Quinn will always be there for you. No matter what happens to your fire station."

Rick looks startled, but just then Quinn comes back into the kitchen.

I pull my hand back, of course, but I'm not quick enough. I can tell by the expression on Quinn's face that he saw me with my hand over Rick's hand. Quinn doesn't say anything, though, and I certainly don't have any words. I settle for a frown instead. The only one in the kitchen looking like they haven't bitten into something sour is Rick. He's looking uncommonly pleased with himself. I should have known better than to try to sympathize with the man.

"I've got to go," I finally say. I've eaten most of my French toast, and I'm not hungry anymore. "Classes."

I take my plate to the sink and then go upstairs to get my books. I slip the Sisterhood journal into my book bag. If I have any time between classes, I plan to write about my upcoming Saturday night. For the first time, I'm glad I'm having that makeover tomorrow. I know Rick and I aren't going out on a real date, but I'd still like to make his jaw drop when he sees how good I can look.

I stand in my doorway and reach in my pocket for my Lizzie stone.

Chapter Three

"Always be a first-rate version of yourself, and not a second-rate version of someone else."

—Judy Garland

Carly was the only one of us who used to worry about her makeup when she was dealing with doctors and tests and the general messiness of having cancer. She's the one who brought us this quote. She said it was important that we be ourselves no matter what happened. This wasn't idle talk. She knew that, during much of that time, each of us sincerely wished we could be almost anyone else.

I used to dream I was a beautiful Russian ballet dancer, but I would have settled for being the quiet girl in math class who sat in the corner and never talked to anyone, not even those of us who tried to talk to her. Being unhappy was better than being sick.

"At least you have natural curls," Carly says as she runs a brush through my hair. I am sitting on a stool beside the Macy's cosmetic counter and my makeover has begun. Carly knows all of the women who work at the counter, so they are letting her take the lead in my transformation.

"It was the cancer," I say without thinking. The closest sales clerk looks at me in alarm and motions something to Carly. It isn't hard to figure out what the sales clerk is upset about. Cancer is bad for business even if the chemo did add the red tones to my hair and gave it more curl than I had before I was sick.

"Of course, that's not a problem now," I add, loud enough so the clerk can hear. My hair is cut short, so it shouldn't take Carly long to smooth it into shape.

"How about this?" Marilee interrupts Carly to show me a tube of eyeliner that she brought back from one of the nearby racks. Macy's has display areas for a dozen different brands of cosmetics. A plain Jane can come in here and, with the right products, leave a glamour queen. "It claims it makes your lashes look like they're bathed in moonlight."

"It smells like seaweed." I open the tube. There is some natural, organic makeup here, and I'm never sure what's in it. "Definitely green."

"They call it sea-gray," Marilee says. "And you want to call attention to your eyes. They're your best feature."

"Men love mysterious eyes," Carly adds, and she stops brushing my hair. Instead, she stares off, sounding like she's dreaming of her own boyfriend, who just happens to have very nice eyes. And they're not even his best feature.

Becca is at the counter across from me, trying to find

the perfect lip gloss. She looks a little lost in thought, too. Her boyfriend is also very nice.

This is pathetic. Everyone in the Sisterhood, except for me, is in a serious relationship. Marilee is with my brother, Quinn, of course. Carly is with Randy Parker, the man who helped out Uncle Lou in the Pews years ago and now has his own diner. Even Becca, who swore she had no time for men, is dating Mark Russo, the guy who runs the homeless shelter for teenagers, where she volunteers as much as she can when she's not studying for her law classes.

I'm the only one who isn't with anyone.

No wonder they're anxious for me to have a boyfriend. We're so used to helping each other get to the next step in our health and careers, I guess it's just natural they all want me to step up to the same romantic level they are on.

"Not everyone needs a man in her life," I say. The same clerk who was alarmed before now looks like she's going to drape a sheet over me. I suppose not looking for a man is as objectionable here as deadly disease is.

"Rick is going to like what he sees," Marilee says soothingly. "Don't worry."

"I'm not worried. I'm just reminding us that not all women live to impress men."

Marilee shrugs. "Of course, there are other things in life, too."

I nod and take a breath. All of the sisters are gathered around me, and now is the time. "That's right. There are other very important things—like finally getting right with God."

I look around me at the faces of my very good

friends. "I'm hoping you will all be in church tomorrow to see me go forward."

It's as quiet as I knew it would be.

Marilee is the first one to grin. "I wouldn't miss it."

"I'll be there," Carly says. She's beaming.

"Me, too," Becca adds.

I think to myself that someone turned the lights on brighter by the cosmetic counter. I know they didn't, but it feels like it.

"I haven't said anything to anyone else," I add with a look to Marilee.

She nods, still beaming . "I'll wait for you to tell your big brother."

The sisters enclose me in a group hug, and Carly decides she needs to make an announcement in our journal. She must have seen the journal tucked into the side of the book bag I carry with me. I give her the journal, and she takes it to an empty space on the counter and opens it to write.

Hi, this is Carly. It's 1:45 in the afternoon of March 17 in Pasadena, California, and hallelujah!! Our sweet Lizabett just told us she wants to be a Christian. I knew God was working in her heart— well, maybe I didn't know it, but I was sure praying for it. None of us wanted to push her; Lizabett needed to make up her own mind about things. If she didn't, she would worry. I wanted to write it all down so we'll remember everything. We're standing around the cosmetic counter at the Macy's on Lake Avenue giving Lizabett a makeover. I guess the symbolism is obvious.

* * *

Carly brings the journal back, and I put it in my book bag again.

The other sisters are still standing close by me and grinning.

"We do have a new lipstick you might like to try," the poor sales clerk finally says timidly from behind the counter.

"I don't know," I say. It seems odd to put makeup on my face when I'm thinking about God.

Apparently Becca has no such hesitation, though. She holds her hand out to the clerk. "Didn't I see something to your left called Passion Pink or Pink Passion—something like that?"

The clerk nods as she pulls open a drawer behind her. "I've got extras here."

"Becca," I protest. "I don't think now's the time for—"

"Now's exactly the time," she says firmly. "God's in the business of miracles. Who knows what He has in store for you and Rick on this date of yours?"

Well, here I am speechless again. The others think that God might care about me and my halfway date. I know He cares about me and the big stuff like my health, but I've never expected any extra effort on my love life. Of course, to be honest—

"It's not really a date," I say. "Rick just wants to discuss a party the fire station is going to have for their lightbulb." I look over at Marilee. "He's in charge of planning a party for the thing. And it's important because their old fire station might not be around forever."

"It doesn't matter what Rick has in his mind now," Marilee says firmly. "It's what he will get in his mind when he sees you that counts."

"When he sees you at your Passion Pink best," Becca adds as she holds up the lip gloss that the clerk just handed her, "he'll forget all about some lightbulb. The thing's so old I hear they have all kind of weird superstitions about it. Like that it will be bad luck if it does go out. I feel like saying, 'Hello, people. Of course, it's going to go out sometime. It's a lightbulb.' That's not bad luck. That's facing reality."

I close my lips, and Becca starts to put the gloss on me.

"Fortunately, you don't have that kind of stuff fogging up your brain," Becca says. "You're sensible."

I wonder how sensible I am when I'm beginning to wonder if God has any way He can make Rick interested in me. Just for a day or two. I'd like to know what it feels like to have him kiss me. One kiss—is that too much to ask? If God can keep a lightbulb going for a hundred years, a kiss shouldn't be too much to ask.

I'm still thinking about God making things sizzle with Rick and me when I'm getting dressed for dinner. I don't do anything to my makeup, since I'm under strict orders not to change anything. I do follow the sisters' instructions and lay out the midnight-blue dress I had forgotten was in the back of my closet. The material has enough spandex in it that it doesn't wrinkle, and it drapes nicely from the shoulders. Its primary job tonight, though, is to draw attention to my eyes.

I look in the mirror. I'm wearing that sea-gray mascara. My eyes generally shift from green to blue depending on what I wear, and this dress and mascara will put them solidly in the blue category. I know Rick likes blue eyes. I stop a moment before I admit to myself the reason I know his preference on so many things.

I'm not proud of it, but I used to keep a tally of Rick's girlfriends. I was much younger at the time, but I did discover that seven out of the ten girlfriends he had back then had blue eyes. Eight of the ten had blond hair. Four of them were English majors. It's depressing that I know that kind of stuff. Even more discouraging, though, was the fact that not one of them was a slight, pixie-faced girl like me.

Turning around, I pick up the dress and let it slip over my shoulders. I check the mirror to be sure that my eyes *have* turned blue. I lean closer to peer into my reflection. I wonder if my eye makeup is too thick. And I have pink gloss over my lip liner, so there is nothing subtle about these lips. I do look older though and more sophisticated than I usually do. And it's good that Rick can clearly see my lips just in case he should get any ideas about kissing them.

I look at the clock on my nightstand. It's time to go downstairs if I want to be in the living room when Rick knocks on the door. Fortunately, my mother is at a friend's house tonight playing bunco, so she won't be here to gaze hopefully at us.

I pick up the book bag that has my wedding brochures in it. If Rick needs any price comparisons for his celebration, I'll have them. When I walk down the stairs, I see that Quinn is sitting in the recliner in the corner of the living room. He frowns a little as he looks up from the sports magazine he's reading. Then he looks at me more closely and frowns some more.

"Shouldn't you wear a jacket over that dress?" he asks.

"I have long sleeves." I turn a little so he can't see the deep vee in the back of the dress. That's the only thing that makes the dress sophisticated, but I know he won't like it. I half suspect he already knows it's there somehow, though. He'd really prefer I draped a flour sack over my head and went out that way.

"And what did you do to your eyes?" Quinn stands up and comes closer.

"Don't be such an Old Mother Hen," I say. That's my nickname for Quinn, and he deserves it tonight for all his fussing. "I'm twenty-two. Old enough to wear makeup."

"Of course, you're old enough," Quinn agrees as he keeps looking at me. "It's just that you don't usually wear much."

I shrug as nonchalantly as I can while still keeping my back to Quinn. "It's only polite to dress up for a Saturday night dinner at the Ritz-Carlton. It's a fancy place. I want to fit in."

Just then there's a knock at the door. I can't answer it, unless I want Quinn to start in again on why I need a jacket to cover my bare back. I don't need to worry, though, because Quinn heads for the door right away.

When Rick steps into the living room, I'm glad the sisters insisted that I wear this dress. He is handsome. He's wearing a dark gray suit. He doesn't have a tie, but I would have looked silly standing next to him wearing something too casual. It'd be like wearing ragged jeans on a date with Cary Grant at his finest.

"I didn't know you were going to the Ritz-Carlton," Quinn says to Rick.

Rick shrugs and grins. "You never asked. Besides, I didn't know you were so interested in my dates."

My pulse jumps a little when he says that. So we *are* on a date.

Quinn grunts. "Just be sure not to keep Lizabett out too late. There's church tomorrow."

I haven't told Quinn about all of my plans for tomorrow, but he's assuming I'll be going with him since I have been doing that lately. Rick's been going to church with my brother, too, but Quinn doesn't mention that to him.

Rick steps over and offers me his arm just like Cary Grant in those old movies.

Once I'm holding Rick's arm, I realize there is no way for me to walk to the door unless I turn my back to my brother. So I figure it's best to do it quickly and get it over with.

"I'll be waiting up," Quinn says grimly as Rick and I step out onto the porch.

"There's no need," I say over my shoulder as the screen door closes behind us.

"I'll leave the porch light on, too," Quinn adds from inside the house.

By now, I am not even paying any attention to my brother. I am walking beside Rick along the brick path leading from my mother's porch to the street. Rick is much taller than I am, but I always knew we would move together in sync like this.

The moon is partially out tonight and the dark air is warm enough that I really don't need a jacket, at least not to protect me from the chill. I probably need more than that to protect me from my imagination, though. It seems to me that Rick just pulled his arm closer to his side, drawing me closer to him. He's wearing an aftershave that smells like the woods, and he knows I love the woods.

"I brought some brochures," I say. I need to stay focused. If I don't, I'll sigh in pure wistfulness.

"What brochures?" Rick says, and his voice is so low it's almost a whisper.

I turn to look up at him before I answer, and I forget everything. The moonlight outlines his jaw, and his eyes are dark in the night.

"The lightbulb," I finally manage to squeak out.

We stop. We are in front of Rick's car and we just stand there. For a second, I think he is going to kiss me. Then a cool breeze drifts by and I shiver a little.

Rick reaches down and opens the car door. "Here, let's get you inside."

I slide into the passenger seat and set my book bag with the brochures at my feet. Maybe Quinn is right. He didn't say it, but I could tell what he was thinking a minute ago. Rick and I have no business going out to dinner at a place like the Ritz-Carlton. We'd be better off going to a drive-in window for hamburgers and eating them on my mother's front porch. That would definitely not be a date.

Rick opens the driver's door and seats himself behind the wheel. I wish I had my Lizzie stone with me. There are no pockets on this dress, though, so I left the rock on my dresser. I guess I'll just have to live with my nerves.

Chapter Four

"No, I don't understand my husband's theory of relativity, but I know my husband and I know he can be trusted."

—Elsa Einstein

Rose brought this quote to the sisterhood several months after we started meeting. She was trying to show us how important trust is. Of course, we didn't trust each other back then, so we didn't totally appreciate the quote. The fact that we were all fighting cancer bound us together from the first, but trust was not automatic. It took time for each of us to realize that the others truly cared about what happened to all of us. Once we knew that, we gave in to trust easily. I've never regretted the commitment I made to the sisters. It's natural to trust people when you know they are as completely in your corner as you are in theirs.

If our waiter, Alfred, wasn't so dignified in his black and white uniform, I would have asked him to pinch my arm. Ever since I waltzed out of my mother's living room on Rick's arm tonight, I've felt like I'm spinning around in a fairytale dream. Of course, I wouldn't be able to smell the roses in the huge bouquet to my right if I wasn't actually sitting in the main dining room at the Ritz-Carlton.

And truthfully, if this was a dream of mine, I wouldn't let that woman on my left be in it. She keeps looking at Rick and then back at me like she can't figure out how I managed to convince someone as handsome as him to be seen in public with me. Of course, if this *is* a dream, she might just be symbolic of my own deep misgivings on the matter. I don't know how I came to be here with him, either.

The Ritz-Carlton is so quiet no one, not even a dreamer, needs to worry about being awakened abruptly. I have never been here before, but Carly and Marilee told me about it while they did my nails yesterday. They didn't mention how the dark polished wood absorbs all of the little sounds of cutlery and conversation, though. Or how the well-dressed and well-moneyed people look so totally natural sitting here. Rick and I are the youngest ones in the place, and neither one of us is close to the income bracket that the other diners appear to fall into effortlessly.

"I've heard the steak here is good," Rick says and then falters. "But I don't see it on the menu."

His voice is low, like he's just as uncomfortable in this place as I am.

If I'd given it a moment's thought, I would have known this isn't his kind of a place, either. Although he does look really good here. I've been trying to figure it out. Maybe it's just the suit. Usually, I see him in his gray jogging outfit—not that he looks bad in that, but here in this setting he's movie-star handsome.

I'm not sure which I prefer. Oh, I know the suit makes him look terrific, but I'm more comfortable with the old gray jogging outfit even if it does have a neck band that is starting to fray and a tiny grease spot in the middle of the back from that time he changed the oil in my car last fall.

The deal is that I know the Rick who wears the jogging outfit, but this suit guy is a little intimidating.

I look back at my menu—and then glance over the top of it so I can keep looking at Rick. I wonder where he's been keeping that suit. And his hair—it looks extra thick. I bet he used mousse on it tonight. And the flickering of the candle on the table makes his chin seem unusually rugged. He sure doesn't look like this when he's sitting at my mom's kitchen table.

I try to focus on the menu. I wish I had asked the sisters what they ordered when they came here. I don't want to order anything too expensive. Rick makes pretty good money as a fireman, but I know he's saving money so he can buy a condo like Quinn's. It would be odd to just order a salad, though. Then I look at the salad prices and cringe. They're steep, too.

"I haven't seen that suit before," I say because I can't think of anything else to talk about and I don't want to keep staring at the gold-embossed menu. Everything's expensive. I can't just order a cup of tea. I do notice that the price they charge for tea here would get me a big bowl of soup at the Pews, though.

"I bought the suit a few days ago," Rick says as he shifts his shoulders like the jacket doesn't fit quite as comfortably as it should. "I decided a man needs a suit in case he wants to—" He pauses.

I freeze. He couldn't possibly have bought a suit to have dinner with me. Could he? If that's what he did, he should have asked first. We didn't need to come to the stuffiest restaurant in Pasadena. Even if he didn't want to go to the Pews because everyone he works with eats there so often, we could have eaten at that Thai place on Colorado Boulevard. I can't believe he'd buy a suit to go out with me.

"Well, I might need it for the lightbulb ceremony," Rick finally finishes. "And I've been going to church with Quinn and—"

"Oh, of course," I say. I'm not sure if I'm relieved or disappointed. I suppose he might need to wear a suit when he presides over the event at the station.

"Quinn said you'd be going to church tomorrow," Rick adds as he looks over at me.

I nod. My walk forward will surprise my brother. I look at Rick; I wonder what he will think of the whole thing.

"Good," Rick says with a nod.

I squint across the table at him. I hope he knows enough not to laugh when I start walking down the aisle. "Church is a serious thing."

"I know," he says so calmly that it's clear to me he doesn't get it at all.

"You shouldn't laugh at people there," I say. I can't make it clearer than that.

"Hey, I'm giving a birthday party for a lightbulb," Rick says with a grin. "I can't afford to laugh at anyone no matter what they do."

"Remember that," I say.

Just then Alfred the waiter comes back. "Can I answer any questions for you?"

He's already brought us a basket of bread and asked for our order twice.

Rick looks up at him with what might be relief. "I don't suppose you have a recommendation."

"The shrimp with fire-roasted garlic is good if you like something that's a little hot," Alfred says. "And the wild Alaskan salmon with the citrus sauce and risotto is the chef's special tonight. That would be my personal preference. They both come with our special Pasadena dinner salad."

Rick lifts his eyebrow in a question to me, and I nod.

"We'll have two of the salmon dinners then," Rick says.

"Excellent choice," Alfred says as he collects our menus.

Now that my menu is gone, I wish I had it back because it gave me something to do with my hands. And then I remember why Rick invited me here. "Would you like to see some of the brochures I brought to help with your party? They're mostly for weddings, but you can look at the catering suggestions and maybe you'll get some ideas for invitations."

"I thought I'd just tack a note on the bulletin board."

"Well, that's one way to do it," I say. It has slowly been occurring to me that this will be good practice for me. And maybe in the future—if there is a future for this fire station—they will want an event planner like me to take on these special events. I could give them a good rate because they're public servants, and it would be excellent advertising for me since I would be able to list them as a client.

I lift my book bag up to my lap and pull out some of the brochures. I started collecting them for my classes before Quinn and Marilee even got engaged. I have all of the wedding chapels around Pasadena as well as fliers from caterers and outdoor furniture rentals and other party stores.

I shuffle through the fliers. "Do you know what kind of food you'd like to have? I've got some names of people who will give you a discount. I have chicken kebabs, gyros, even hamburgers. Or something more historic—you know, to go with the year the lightbulb was turned on. I don't know what they were eating back then in firehouses, but we can do whatever you want."

I pull out a green sheet that lists my catering contacts before I look up and see Rick staring at me like I've just grown another head.

"You're really serious about this," he finally says, clearly surprised. "I didn't know we even had that many things related to weddings around here."

I look down at my brochures and see that most of them do have bridal photos on them—cakes, flowers, that sort of thing.

"Of course, I'm serious," I say with a little heat. "People trust their wedding planner with the most important day in their life. I can't just make things up as I go along."

"No, I suppose you can't," he says, and I think there's a new note of respect in his voice.

"A wedding sets the stage for a good marriage," I explain. I dare him to show any sign of amusement. "I know a lot of men would agree with Quinn that city hall or a pastor's study does just fine, but that's only the legal side of it. There needs to be room for the heart to speak as well. It all needs to mean something and make memories."

Rick holds up his hands in surrender. "You won't get any argument from me. My parents got married in a judge's office someplace. My mother used to throw that in my father's face when she was mad. She didn't have a wedding dress or a bouquet or anything. If they'd cared from the beginning, maybe they would have stuck together longer. They would have been better off going to Vegas—at least there they might have gone to one of those wedding chapels and had something to look back on."

Just then Alfred is back with our salads.

"Oh, excuse me," I say as I start to pick up the brochures so Alfred can set the salad plates down.

"There's no problem," Alfred says, his voice warmer than it has been all evening. "I like to see a young couple planning their wedding."

I stop stacking the brochures and look up at Alfred. He's smiling because he thinks— "Oh, no—I—we're not. I mean we're not planning a wedding—it's for—ah—for a birthday celebration. Sort of."

I spare our waiter the knowledge that the guest of honor will be an old lightbulb. I'm not sure he'd understand.

Alfred frowns a little as he sets our salads on the table. "That's too bad." The waiter looks down at Rick. "A man needs a good wife."

"Yes, he does," Rick says right back to the waiter without missing a beat.

I look over at Rick, expecting to see amusement in his eyes, but there's none.

Alfred nods his approval. "Would either of you like some pepper on your salad?"

He holds up the grinder, but we both shake our heads.

I wait for Alfred to leave and then start putting the brochures back in my book bag. "Sorry about that. I should have just told him about the lightbulb."

"And ruin his night?" Rick says. "He wants to play matchmaker. Besides, he's right about marriage being good for a man."

I look up. That doesn't sound like someone who used to change girlfriends more frequently than most people change the months on their calendars.

"You?" I can't help but ask.

"What?" Rick gives a quick grin. "I'm serious. Have you seen how happy Quinn is these days? I never used to envy him. He always seemed weighted down with the troubles in your family after your father died. But in the last year or so—" Rick spreads his hands "—he's become a truly happy man."

"I never liked to see him so worried, either," I say. Quinn has been a substitute father to me and my two other brothers since he was nine. He stopped worrying about my brothers, but he still frets over me because I'm the youngest. "I think he suffered as much as I did when I had cancer."

"Those days were difficult for all of us."

"Oh." It never occurred to me that Rick would have been affected by my cancer. "It must have been hard to see your good friend so worried."

Rick gives me an odd look, but he doesn't say anything.

We're silent for a minute or two, and then I say, "Fortunately, things are better now."

Rick nods. I glance over his shoulder and see that the woman is still watching us. I sit up straighter. What does she know? She may disapprove all she wants, but Alfred thought Rick would be fortunate to have me for a wife. And it's clear that Alfred is a man of discriminating taste even if he doesn't have much of a sense of whimsy.

Our salads are sitting in front of us, but neither one of us picks up a fork.

Rick finally looks over at me and grins. He holds his hand out across the table. "I'll say grace for us."

"What?"

I look at his hand for a moment. I can't quite believe he's offering to say a blessing over the food. I don't think he's ever prayed in his life. At least, not to God. I know he's been going to church, but it's not serious.

"No buzzer," he says when I keep hesitating. He spreads the fingers in his hand so I can see there's nothing hidden. "I promise."

He and Quinn both loved practical jokes when they were in junior high. I suddenly wonder if that's why he's so fascinated with that lightbulb. It's a mechanical oddity. If it only made some kind of humming noise or zapped people, it would be perfect.

"You volunteered, didn't you?" I ask. "To be responsible for that lightbulb?"

Rick shrugged. "It was Quinn or me, and he's got enough to think about with the—"

"Don't say it."

"Sorry. It's not the getting married part. He wants to do that. It's just the—"

"I know what it's *just,*" I say. "But I don't think

Marilee should have to give up her dreams of the perfect wedding because she's marrying a man who doesn't have a romantic thought in his head."

"Hey, don't kill the messenger," Rick says as he smiles at me. "I'm only trying to pray here."

There's not much I can say to that. So I reach out and take his hand. "Well, let's do it then."

We both bow our heads, and I wonder if Rick does have some device between his fingers. My hand feels warm inside his, and the restaurant is on the chilly side.

Before I know it, the prayer is over and I didn't really hear anything Rick said. He could have been complaining about the salad for all I know.

"Seriously. Marriage will be good for Quinn," Rick says as he frowns down at his salad, which contains endive and a few other things he's probably reluctant to eat.

"There's alfalfa sprouts in it, too," I say as I use my fork to pick up some of the salad. "Quinn wouldn't like it, either."

"Well, a man doesn't need to eat exotic food to be a good man," Rick says.

"Fortunately for you," I reply.

We silently eat our salads for a minute or two. I try to look blissful as I chew the alfalfa sprouts even though I must admit they are a little twiggy.

"Do you have a budget for your party?" I finally ask.

"Yeah, we have some money," Rick says. "But it's not enough."

"I know what you mean," I say as I set my fork back on my plate. "It's the never-ending problem of the wedding planner."

"Having problems keeping costs down with Quinn's wedding?"

"I'm having problems because he wants them practically at zero," I say. "And there's the flowers at the altar, the pictures, the reception, the—"

Rick interrupts. "Well, couldn't we do some of that ourselves?"

"We?"

"Yeah," Rick says. "I'm glad to help with anything. You just let me know."

"Oh," I say. I wonder if my face looks as surprised as my insides are feeling. "You don't have to do that. I have contacts because of the classes I'm taking. Coupons. Freebies. Favors. I'm sure I'll manage fine—"

"Well, if it doesn't work out that way, I'm happy to help."

"I don't think—" I say.

"Look, you can help me with my celebration," Rick says. "That is, if you want to. I'll help with the wedding regardless."

"Really?"

"I'm the best man. The least I can do is help with the thing. I'm sure you need a lot of—well—stuff done. Putting ribbons on posts or something."

I'm silent for a second or two, but then I just can't stand it. "What's happened to you? I can't believe you're volunteering to tie ribbons anywhere. You've never liked anything like that."

"A man can change," Rick says firmly. "In fact, it's good to change some."

There doesn't seem to be much I can say to that. "Well, I'll certainly keep that in mind. Thank you."

He nods.

Fortunately, I won't need to ask for Rick's help. Besides, planning this fantasy wedding is something I want to do to prove to everyone that I can. I made a commitment to Quinn and Marilee; I don't want to be rescued because I'm falling down on the job. I've been rescued too many times in my life. It's time I stood on my own.

For the rest of the evening, I keep waiting for Rick to announce he's been playing an April Fool's joke or something, even though he'd be a month early and I doubt even a dedicated practical joker would be willing to spend the kind of money he did tonight for a joke that didn't have much of a punch line.

Before I know it, I am walking back down the brick sidewalk toward the door of my mother's house. This time Rick has his arm around my shoulders and I am trying to think of a reason for us to make a detour around the block before we get to the porch.

The night has turned even cooler, and there is a full moon in the sky. Even with the chill, I am grateful for the deep vee in the back of my dress because I can feel Rick's arm across my shoulders.

"Does Quinn know your worries about the lightbulb celebration?" I ask when we're halfway to the door. I figure Rick might want to stop and chat for a while and that's the best I can come up with for a topic. I'd talk about the bricks beneath our feet if it would get him to slow down as we walk toward the porch.

"Quinn doesn't need to know everything," Rick says, but he keeps on walking.

"Really?" I thought Rick told Quinn everything. This evening is becoming more and more bizarre.

Before I can think of anything else to prolong the evening, we are stepping up to the porch. Thankfully, the light is out. I'm sure Quinn left it on, but maybe the bulb had the decency to burn out on its own. Rick still has his arm around me, and I hold my breath when he slowly turns to look at me fully.

"I had a nice time tonight," he says. "Thanks."

I nod and murmur an agreement of some sort.

This is the moment I've been waiting for. I know Rick is going to kiss me. We're standing there facing each other in the dark, him in his suit and me in my midnight-blue dress with the plunging back. I am glad the sisters insisted I have a makeover today. I know I am looking as close to radiant as I've ever looked in my life. I am ready for romance.

Rick is gazing at me with eyes filled with fondness, and he bends down.

I start to close my eyes. Here it comes—the kiss.

Then I feel his lips. *On my forehead?*

My eyes fly open. He kissed me on my forehead!

And there's light. Some time in all of this my brother opened the door to the house. He's standing inside and looking through the screen door and the light is streaming out from behind him.

"Good. You got home early," Quinn says as he waves at Rick, who is already starting to turn so he can go back down the steps. "See you tomorrow."

"Well," I say even though I don't have anything to follow it up with. A kiss on the forehead is as brotherly as a kiss can be. My dreams deflate like a pricked balloon.

I watch Rick walk back to his car before I turn to my brother. "Were you watching us?"

Quinn's face pinks up. "I heard something outside, and I thought I should check it out. It could have been a stray pet or something. Or even a coyote. I've heard there were a few coyotes coming down from the San Gabriels. That could be dangerous."

"I don't need to worry about any coyotes." I stomp into the house and turn to my brother. I cross my arms. "Not when I have you around."

"I was only checking out the porch," he says. "The light had burned out."

"That lightbulb is always burning out," I say in irritation. "That's not the point. You're still supposed to give me some privacy on a date." I may never have another chance to get a kiss from Rick. "I don't interrupt you and Marilee—not even when it's totally dark on the porch and—"

I see right away that I've made a mistake. "Not that Rick and I are serious like you and Marilee are. We're just making plans for that party at your station house."

"The One Hundred and Five thing?" Quinn asks. "If that's what you were talking about, you don't need any privacy. The more people who know about that party, the better. Rick is trying to get the *Star News* to come. So far he doesn't have any takers, but he's hoping some woman he knows there will cover the thing if he chats her up a bit."

So Rick has told Quinn all about the troubles with the celebration, after all. I'm not even special in that regard.

On that depressing note, I tell my brother good-night and walk up the stairs to my bedroom. My mother has probably been asleep for an hour already. I look out the window in my room. The moon is still up; it's not that dark outside. I should have known it was too much to ask that my date would go as I had secretly wished. All I really wanted was a full-blown kiss.

I walk over to my nightstand to pick up the Lizzie stone. I absentmindedly rub it for a while. It apparently works for sadness as well as worry.

Chapter Five

"I want to live my life, not record it."
—Jacqueline Kennedy Onassis

Becca brought this quote one evening along with a helium balloon for each of us. She always did believe in living life first and then thinking about it afterward. I've often wondered if all the knitting we do is too slow for her. She never says anything, but she is always the one who encourages us to set short-term goals and work hard to meet them. A quick-rising balloon is more her style than the slow progress of knitting needles.

I've always thought her determination is what helped us get better as fast as we did. When she said it was time to march, we didn't hesitate. We just put one foot in front of the other and moved ahead. None of us had time to worry about whether we would stumble tomorrow when we had so much trouble just keeping ourselves going on the day we had in front of us.

* * *

I am sitting in the pew between Carly and Becca. Marilee e-mailed me this morning saying that she was sick and couldn't make it to church. I am disappointed but am glad I had told her yesterday what I was going to do. It makes me feel like she is with me in some way even if she is home in bed.

I had hoped to be sitting at the end of the pew, but before Carly could change with me, Quinn and Rick came to sit with us and I didn't want to explain why I wanted to sit on the outside edge so I am now three people from the end.

But it's not a problem. A dozen people could be sitting between me and the aisle and it wouldn't stop me. I am focusing on the moment when the pastor will ask people to come forward if they want to belong to Jesus. I am a little nervous. But it's in a good way, like I'm going to run a marathon and am waiting for the starting gun to sound.

Everyone stands to sing "Amazing Grace," and I start to number my blessings as I sing along. At the top of my list today is that I have been led to this church. When we sit back down, I try to listen to the sermon but fail miserably. Most of the time I am thinking about what it will feel like to march up to the altar. I promise myself I will check out an audio cassette of this morning's sermon and listen to it at home this week.

It's probably because of my distractions that I don't notice that Rick is wearing his suit this morning. Of course, even if I had really seen the suit, I wouldn't have ever suspected what it meant.

Pastor Engstrom is right on time with his invitation

to come forward. He says the words just like he told me he would when I talked to him about it on Wednesday. I take a deep breath, preparing to stand up.

Before I can get to my feet, though, Rick is standing up. At first, I wonder if he knows I'm going to go forward and he's rising to his feet so I can get out of the pew easier. I marvel at how that suit has turned him into a regular gentleman. But then I notice that he's not standing at the end of the pew waiting for me to come out. He's not being polite at all; he's walking to the front just like I'm supposed to be doing.

Hey, wait!

I get to my feet, even though I'm not having the pious moment I thought I would. There are no angels whispering in my ears or anything tingling in my spine. Mostly what I feel is bewilderment about Rick. I've known him all of my life, and I never thought he would do something like this to me—or anyone else, either.

Although what exactly he's doing I'm not quite sure.

I glance down at Quinn while I squeeze by him so I can exit the pew. He's not holding back laughter or anything, so Rick must not be playing a practical joke. The two of them were always in on each other's jokes. Besides, I don't see how this could be funny.

Oh. It finally hits me. Rick is going forward for himself.

I hear a grunt behind me as I step out in the aisle. It sounds like Quinn had the breath knocked out of him. He must be as surprised about Rick as I am. By now, Rick is several yards ahead of me. There are a couple of people in other parts of the church who are walking forward, but I only see Rick.

I wonder if he knows what he's doing.

I wanted this to be a pious moment. Instead, all I can get my mind around is that people will think I'm following Rick to the altar like those women who walk two steps behind their men. How pathetic does that look? Granted, there was a day when I would have followed him anywhere, but that was when I was seven. I haven't trailed after him like this for years, well, not much.

I want people to know that my decision is for me and me alone.

When I arrive at the altar, I stand as far away from Rick as I can. Pastor Engstrom comes over to pray with me and I notice that one of the associate pastors goes over to pray with Rick.

As Pastor Engstrom starts talking to me, I forget about being annoyed with Rick. I have already made my mind up, so it feels natural to repeat the words of my new faith as Pastor Engstrom guides me. It doesn't take much time at all to do.

I must admit I am happy—and, for the first time, I'm not worried that something bad will happen because of it.

Then Pastor Engstrom is leading everyone in a prayer together, and when he finishes the organist starts playing some joyful song. I turn to look at the people sitting in the pews, and I see that my brother has tears on his face. That makes me want to cry, too.

"You don't need to worry," I say to Quinn as soon as people start moving around and I can walk back to the pew. "I'm sure Rick didn't know—"

"This isn't about Rick," my brother says as he opens his arms. "Come here."

I know my brother shed some tears over me when I had cancer. I didn't expect these, though.

I can see out of the corner of my eyes that Becca is hugging Rick, and then Quinn loosens his hold on me and he's hugging Rick and Carly is hugging me. I ask myself how I feel because I want to remember and write it down in the journal. And then——I don't know how it happened——but this merry-go-round of hugs lands me in Rick's arms.

"Oh," I say. My voice is muffled since my face is pressed against his suit-covered shoulder.

"I had no idea," Rick whispers against my ear. Well, maybe he's whispering it more against the hair on the top of my head. "I didn't know you were——"

"I've been meeting with the pastor," I manage to mumble. "Privately."

"Me, too," he says, and I feel his hands holding my head. Then he's kissing the top of my head.

Oh, well. This time I don't mind so much that he's giving me a brotherly kiss. I can't believe we both became Christians on the same day. What are the odds? I can tell by the happy chatter all around that no one thinks I followed Rick up to the altar just because he was headed in that direction.

Everyone is so keyed up that, when Quinn suggests we go out to eat, we all agree. No one really suggests the Pews. It's just kind of understood that, when we say we'll meet, the Pews is where we'll go. Carly gave me a ride to church, and the two of us walk back to where she's parked.

I left the Sisterhood journal on the seat of her car when we went into church earlier, so I pick it up before I slide into the passenger seat. I open it up and look over as Carly settles herself with her seat belt.

"Can I take a minute?" I ask.

"Of course," she says.

I unclip the pen that I had put with the journal earlier and begin to write.

I did it. And there was no weird physical reaction. I did cry a little, but that was mostly because I saw my brother's tears. It felt good, though. Not floaty or anything, but like it was safe to be happy—that I didn't have to worry that something bad would happen in response to this wonderful feeling.

The rest of what I have to say can wait. I just wanted to get the initial reaction down on paper. I close the journal and re-clip the pen.

"Thanks," I say to Carly, and she starts up her car's engine.

Carly gets on the 210 Freeway and starts back to Pasadena. She tells me a dozen times how excited she is for me on the way to the parking structure on Raymond Avenue.

We start walking down Colorado Boulevard toward the Pews, and before I know it, we are almost at the old fire station where Quinn and Rick work.

As we start to pass the brick building Carly stops to look. There are windows along the top of the building. "Do you think we can see the lightbulb from out here?"

I shake my head. "I'm not sure they can see it very well when they're right under it. The thing's only four watts. It started out as a night-light. And no one even dusts it anymore because they're afraid they might break it. I think they've been keeping that fire station open just because of the beam holding that lightbulb."

"I can't believe it's still going after all that time." Carly stands on her tiptoes as though that will make her able to see in those high windows. When she can't see anything, she lowers her heels and turns to me. "Are you going to the party?"

I shrug. "Maybe. I might help Rick with some of the planning."

"Really." Carly's eyes get big. "That could be fun."

"Well, they want to save the fire station, too, so it's a big deal," I say, and we start walking again. We're so distracted neither one of us looks at the sign in the gelato store window to see what kind of fresh fruit topping is on special today.

The front area of the Pews is packed with people having lunch so we head for the Sisterhood room. We don't usually invite anyone else to eat in the room with us, but today is clearly an exceptional day.

Rick and Quinn enter the Pews behind us, and we motion for them to follow.

"Wow," Rick says when he walks into the back room. "I never thought I'd get invited into the secret sanctuary."

"It's just a room," I say as I pull out some chairs for people to sit on.

"No, it's not," Rick says quietly as he sits down in the chair next to me. "It's part of what helped you get better."

I notice he doesn't say the cancer word. Quinn doesn't, either. None of us like to think of those years.

"You should have come around here earlier," Carly says from where she's sitting across the table. "There's great food out front. And coffee, too."

"I thought I'd wait for an invitation," Rick says as he gives me a quick look.

I just stare at him. I was supposed to invite him? "It's a public place."

"Well, you didn't want Quinn to come, so I thought—" His voice trailed off. "Anyway, I didn't want to make you feel like you didn't have your own place. I know how important that was to you."

"You're always welcome here," I say softly.

Rick smiles at me, a real no-holding-back grin of affection. I'm tempted to try and figure out if it's brotherly love or maybe a little more, but then I decide just to let the moment be what it is. Affection is good.

How many more wonderful surprises can today hold? I plan to just sit back and enjoy them with no twinge of anxiety.

I look away from Rick and see that Becca is coming in the door, followed by Shelley, the waitress who is working today. Uncle Lou always hires college students to wait tables, and I know Shelley from my classes at PCC. Technically, the waitresses don't have to take orders in this back room, but they do it for us when they can.

"Is everyone ready to order?" Shelley asks.

We all have our favorites, so the ordering goes fast, even for Rick who isn't familiar with the menu but only wants a hamburger.

There is so much contentment in the room I can't help but wish again that Marilee were here sharing it all with us. I don't want to disturb her when she's sick by calling her on her cell phone, but I decide it would be nice to leave a note on her door so that, when she comes in to her office tomorrow, she will know that I was thinking of her when we were all together.

"I'll be back in a second," I say as I grab my purse and stand up.

I slip through the French doors and walk through the main part of the diner to get to the long hallway that leads down to Marilee's office. I have the Sisterhood journal in my purse and the pen is still attached. I figure I'll tear out one of the pages from the back of the journal and use that for my note. We probably won't use all of the pages in the journal anyway.

I have the piece of paper up against the door of Marilee's office when I hear the soft sounds of someone crying on the other side.

I knock softly. "Marilee?"

The sobbing stops.

"Marilee?" I turn the knob enough to know the door isn't locked. But even if it isn't locked, it's an invasion of privacy to just burst into someone's office no matter how worried I might be.

"Go away," Marilee finally says from inside the room. Her voice sounds weary and profoundly sad.

I can't help myself. I turn the knob and open the door.

"What's wrong?" I ask. Marilee is sitting at her desk wearing one of her old flannel shirts and a baseball cap. Her hair is squashed down and she's not wearing any of the makeup she usually has on these days. "If you're still not feeling good, I could drive you home."

"I just came from home."

"Well, you should be back in bed resting."

Because of the cap, I can't see most of Marilee's

face. I watch as she reaches up a hand and wipes away some tears. Once I see the hand, everything feels like it goes in slow motion. Marilee isn't wearing her engagement ring. I was wrong when I decided nothing bad would happen even with all the good of today. I have a feeling something is terribly wrong.

"Did Quinn do something?" I ask.

Marilee shakes her head. "I just can't get married right now."

I reach for the pocket of my jacket, and then I realize I didn't put the Lizzie stone there when I left my bedroom this morning. I thought I didn't need it any longer. But I was wrong. I wish I had it with me.

"Does Quinn know?"

Marilee shakes her head again. "Can you tell him for me?"

I take a step forward, but Marilee holds up a hand to stop me.

"I don't even know what's wrong," I say. "I wouldn't know what to tell him. And it's not my place."

"You're the wedding planner." Marilee's voice is muffled.

"I don't think that's the job of the—" I begin, but then I pause. "I'll do anything I can to help you feel better. But I know Quinn, and if I go out there and tell him something like this, he'll break this door down so he can talk to you."

"I can't talk to him yet," she says. "Don't tell him I'm back here."

Marilee looks up at me for the first time. Her eyes are still in shadow, but I can see the misery and pleading on her face.

I don't care if she's ready for me to come closer or not. I cross the room to where she's sitting on her desk chair and put my arms around her. "I won't say anything to anyone if you don't want me to."

I feel her shake as her sobs start again. Tears are running down my face by now as well. "You're sure you don't want to talk to Quinn? He loves you. Whatever the problem is, the two of you can fix it. But you can't just not talk to him."

"I've told everyone I'm sick," Marilee says. "I'll just say I have laryngitis."

"If you're sick, you shouldn't be here," I say. I can't tell if she's running a fever or not. Her face is red, but that could be from the tears.

"I needed a baseball cap," Marilee says. "To cover my head."

I hold Marilee until she wears herself out from crying.

"You better go back or someone will come looking for you," Marilee finally says. "I'll just sit in here until all of you leave."

"I'm coming to see you tomorrow," I say. "Maybe after a good night's sleep, you'll be ready to talk."

Marilee gives me a hint of a smile. "Maybe."

"Here, you might want this." I put the Sisterhood journal on the corner of her desk. We all love the journal, but it's Marilee's particular joy. If she can write in it, she might find some peace and be able to talk to Quinn.

With that, I leave her and go back to the Sisterhood room. Everyone has gotten their food and has almost finished eating.

"Celebrating without us?" Rick asks as I sit down in my chair.

I shake my head. "I just kind of—" I let my voice trail off.

"Don't tell me you're sick, too?" Quinn says. "There must be something going around. First Marilee and then you."

I don't know what to say, so I nod. "I think I'll just box up my salad to go."

"I can take you home if you want," Rick offers.

"That would be nice," I say.

By the time we get home, I am feeling unsteady. I put my salad in the refrigerator and go up to my bedroom. The Lizzie stone is sitting on my nightstand where I left it. I sit down on the bed and pick up the stone so I can hold it tight. I have a feeling deep down that someone close to me is going to pay the price for my happiness after all. I know that, now that I'm a Christian, I shouldn't feel a tug for that old piece of rock. But I do.

Chapter Six

"I'm not afraid of storms, for I'm learning how to sail my ship."

—Louisa May Alcott

There is no lack of courage in hospitals. Our counselor, Rose, gave us this quote during one particularly difficult time. None of us seemed to be getting better. Even Becca had given up the inspiring, rah-rah speeches. It felt like we had used everything up and all we had left was some thin core of courage that gave us the ability to face each day. It was so hard to hang on in those months that I wonder if any of us could do it again if we needed.

I think back to that quote while I lie on my bed. My mother sometimes takes a Sunday afternoon nap, and I hope Quinn believes that's what I'm doing today, as well. I'm afraid to face him because I don't want to betray Marilee's trust. Also, whatever the problem is, I want to give Marilee time to find the words to tell Quinn about it herself.

I have no desire to take messages back and forth between the two of them—especially if they are breaking up.

I almost keep the Lizzie stone in my hand when I lay down, but instead I push it back farther on my nightstand. It's going to have to stay there until I can figure out what to do with it. Even if it doesn't seem right for me to hold it now like I did before, I can't just throw it out like it's trash. I need to find someplace special to leave it.

Without the stone, I have nothing to temper my worry, so I turn my face resolutely to the wall. The beige paint I see there should help me stay calm; there can't be much to fret over if I concentrate on beige. In a few minutes, I hope to be able to pray.

I'm trying to distract myself. I refuse to say the one word, even silently, that I fear. At the edge of my mind though, I can't help but wonder. All of the sisters think about it once in a while, even if we don't talk about it very often.

I screw up my courage and flex my fingers; I resist the urge to turn around and reach for my stone again. This can't be that bad. It can't be about cancer.

For the first time, I feel relief at the missing ring on Marilee's finger. The ring means Quinn must have done some insensitive guy thing. It's not her birthday, but maybe he missed some anniversary that only the two of them know about. People in love always have these little secret days. Maybe this is their anniversary of the first time he kissed her and usually he gives her a rose, but today he forgot.

I sigh a little. At least Marilee got kissed—on the lips and not the forehead. I should remind her of that tomorrow. A good kiss can heal a thousand hurt feelings. Especially because I know Quinn loves her deeply. I'm sure if Marilee just told Quinn why she took her ring off, he would explain everything and all would be back to normal.

It would certainly be better than me saying anything to him.

I turn to look at the clock on my nightstand and note that enough time has passed that I can go downstairs. Quinn's shift at the station starts at five, so he would have left the house by now. Which means I can eat some of that salad I was too upset to even touch for lunch.

I brush my hair quickly. Before I leave my room, I pick up the Lizzie stone and put it in the pocket of my sweater. Maybe after I eat, I'll go outside and find someplace to put the stone.

I try to be quiet as I go down the stairs because my mother's door is still closed. When I get to the kitchen, I pick up the container of salad from the refrigerator. I don't feel like sitting inside, so I decide to go outside on the porch and eat in case the birds come early.

I love to wait for the birds. The wild green parrots that fly around Pasadena have started visiting my mother's street about this time every day. They like to roost in the silver maple trees here. The parrots always make a terrible racket, but I've been fascinated with them. They have a lovely history. Back in the late fifties, they escaped from a pet store when it caught on fire. On that day, they went from being well-fed pets to wild birds that needed to learn how to survive in city streets.

Whenever I think of them, it reminds me I'm not the only one who has to adapt.

I open the main house door and start to push against the screen door, when—*oh*—I stop.

I gulp. "I didn't expect to see you here."

I finish opening the screen door and step through.

Rick looks up at me and smiles. He's sitting on the top step and has been reading that same sports magazine Quinn had last night. The late afternoon sun is hitting the porch and it makes Rick's brown eyes look almost golden. His suit jacket is draped over one of the lawn chairs at the top of the porch, and he has the sleeves on his shirt rolled up. He looks relaxed. Much more comfortable than me and much too handsome to see me in my old sweater. Not that he hasn't seen me looking the way I do now a million times before.

"Have the birds come?" I ask. There's a walnut tree in Rick's backyard next door that is particularly popular with the parrots. They also like any berry bushes around.

He shakes his head. "Not while I've been here."

If he wasn't still wearing the same clothes he wore to church, I would have thought he'd gone home to change. He moved back in with his father some months ago so he could save money for the condo he plans to buy soon.

"You've been here this whole time?" I ask.

"I wanted to be sure you were feeling all right," he says. The clouds shift, and shadows cover his face. His eyes are now a deep brown, but he looks away from me. "Quinn needed to leave and—"

I'm suddenly thinking back to all the times that Rick has been around when no one else was there to help. "My brother asked you to wait, didn't he?"

Rick looks up at me, a little sheepish. "I wanted to read some of the articles in this magazine anyway. And it's nice sitting here on the porch. It hasn't been a problem for me to stay."

"Well, it should be a problem—I mean you have a life and you can't be—" I stop and suddenly realize. "You've been doing this for years, haven't you? Babysitting me when Quinn can't."

I need to sit down. I can't sit on the same step as Rick, though—not now—so I pull one of the old lawn chairs over and sink down into its webbed seat. I put my salad container on the wide porch railing to my right. I wish I could put my heart somewhere, too, so it wouldn't keep beating so fast inside me.

I look over and see Rick watching me cautiously.

"I had lots of time back then," he finally says. "Besides, your mom fed me. I owed your whole family."

I keep rolling back the years. "That time you came and helped me with the ballet moves. You hadn't really come by to see Quinn—you were there checking on me."

Rick's eyes flash a little. "Well, I didn't think Quinn and your mom should have both been gone at the same time. You could have fallen, and no one would have even known. Of course, I checked on you."

I sit there absorbing what he's saying.

"Trust me. I didn't mind," Rick finally adds softly. "You were my little Lizzie and you were sick."

I can feel the tears gathering in my eyes. "I'm sorry. I had no idea."

I begin to stand so I can go back inside, but Rick rises at the same time and takes the step up to the porch so that we're even.

"Hey," he says quietly as he puts his hand on my shoulder. "There's no need to apologize. There's nothing wrong with needing help from a friend."

"But I kicked you in the shins," I say. I wipe away the tear that is running down my cheek.

"Well, yeah," Rick says with a chuckle. "But it was only that one time, and I probably deserved it."

"*Probably?* You broke my poor heart."

"I was a foolish young boy back then who didn't know better," Rick says as he takes a step closer and gives me a hug. "It won't happen again."

It's strange how my tears stop when Rick hugs me. He's got that woodsy smell to him, and his arms feel good wrapped around me.

"You're promising never to laugh at me again?" I ask skeptically.

"I'm promising never to break your heart again," Rick says and kisses the top of my head. Which sort of cracks my heart a tiny bit right then and there.

"How old am I?" I ask Rick, my head pressed against his shirt. I can't help but strain to hear if his heart is beating fast like mine is, but all I hear is the steady thump of a man's heart who is hugging someone he thinks of as his little sister.

"Why?" Rick leans back, his voice filled with surprise. "It's not your birthday."

I step back some, too. "No, that's not until November."

"You're not worried about growing old, are you? You're barely out of high school. Why, I still have Girl Scout cookies in my freezer that I bought from you not that long ago."

I look up at his dear puzzled face and feel my heart

break completely in two. I had always thought that maybe when I turned twenty-one Rick would see me as a woman instead of a younger sister. But I'm twenty-two, and if he hasn't figured out that I'm grown by now, he probably never will.

"It's been at least nine years. I don't think cookies last that long," I finally manage to say. "Not even in the freezer."

"I'm saving them for a special occasion," he says.

"I find that hard to believe."

"What?" Rick looks at me. "Even a guy like me is going to have something to celebrate sooner or later."

"Well, yeah but—" I look at him skeptically. "Wait a minute. You celebrate all the time. What are you really saving those cookies for?"

Rick flushes and then grins. "Okay, maybe for a while I was keeping them so when people came over and looked in my freezer they'd see proof that I'm a good guy. Everybody should support the Girl Scouts. They're practically a national institution."

"You're using those cookies to impress women, aren't you?" I say indignantly. "The cookies *I* sold to you."

Rick shrugs.

"Someday you're going to break a tooth on one of those cookies," I say, thinking I've made my point, even if he is standing there grinning at me.

"What?" I snap at him as I reach back and grab my salad container.

"Nothing. I was just thinking how perfect you're going to be as a wedding planner. Nothing gets past you. And you're good with people. You'll do a great job on this wedding for your brother."

"I don't know. So far I haven't even convinced the bride to wear—"

I stop. I almost told him that Marilee is refusing to wear her engagement ring. My only excuse is that Rick sometimes makes me forget my common sense—

"So—" I try to think of something to distract Rick before that thoughtful look on his face turns to an enlightened one "—want some of my salad? I haven't eaten any of it yet, and it's almost too big for one person anyway. If I know you, you're hungry about now. And you should at least have some of that iced tea Mom has in the refrigerator. It's the raspberry-flavored stuff."

There. I've given him all the distractions I can think of. And it works.

"Sure. I could eat," Rick says as he reaches up high enough to pull open the screen door and still leave enough room for me to walk under his arm.

"Good," I say as I duck down low so that I won't touch him as I pass.

I hear the hard thud of something in my pocket hitting the doorjamb before I realize that could be a problem. The pocket of my sweater swings a little.

"What's that?" Rick asks. "A bottle of medicine or something?"

"It's nothing," I say vaguely as I walk into the living room.

"A spoon for cough syrup?"

"I'm not sick," I say. "It's nothing."

"It sounded like a chunk of concrete," Rick says as he follows me through the living room. Then he stops, and I'm fool enough to turn around to see why.

"You still have that rock, don't you?" he asks.

"Quinn said you'd kept it, but that's got to be—what—how many years ago was that?"

"Well, you have those cookies," I say as I turn around and continue walking into the kitchen. If Rick wants any salad, he will just have to pick his jaw up from the floor and follow me.

I stop and get two plates and forks on my way to the table. I spread the salad on the plates, making sure to divide the shrimp and lettuce evenly. I know Rick doesn't like avocados, so I take all of them and give him the tomatoes.

"You'll be happy," I say as he sits down. "There's no alfalfa sprouts."

"I can eat alfalfa sprouts if I have to," Rick says a little defensively.

"Good," I say as I sit down, too. "Because that's probably what those cookies that are in your freezer taste like."

Rick looks at me a minute, and then he grins. "We're a pair, aren't we?"

I don't know what to say to that, so I look down at my salad.

Rick doesn't say anything, he just reaches out his hand. "We need to pray."

I reach over and take his hand. Rick turns his palm slightly so my hand is all swallowed up in his. He seems content for us to just stay this way for a minute.

"I never thought you would be going forward this morning," Rick finally says. "If I'd known, I would have waited for you and we could have walked up together."

Is it my imagination, or is he holding my hand for real and not just for prayer?

I swallow. "I didn't tell anyone I was going to do it—well, except for Pastor Engstrom and the sisters."

Rick nods and bows his head.

I close my eyes and bend my head forward.

"Thank you, Father," Rick prays. "You've given us so much today. Make us worthy of You. Amen."

We both open our eyes and raise our heads, but neither one of us is inclined to pull our hands apart. Rick is just gazing at me with fondness in his eyes. Finally, I'm the one who looks away. Affection will never be enough when I want heart-melting love.

And then Rick starts talking like nothing unusual is happening, so I decide that must be the way it is. After a while the conversation drifts to the One Hundred and Five Celebration.

"You're having it at the fire station, aren't you?" I ask.

Rick nods. "But I don't know if we should have it on the second floor where the lightbulb is—that's where some of the cots are. Or, if we should have it in that newer building, the one beside the old station. But that doesn't help recognition for the old building. We even have a huge tent top we can set up in the back."

"I think either one of them would be fine." I've been in that turn-of-the-century fire station a few times when I've dropped things off for Quinn. It's actually quite attractive with all its polished wood and high windows. I'm sure it's hard to maintain, though, and the building next door is more practical.

"Which do you think would be better for taking pictures?" Rick asks. "The media is still dragging their feet, and I want to make the whole thing as publicity friendly as possible. There's not very good lighting upstairs, but that's where the bulb is." Rick stops and looks at me. "You'll need to come and help me decide. You're the professional. I should just rely on your opinion."

"Technically," I stall, "I'm not exactly a professional yet. The wedding will be my first event and—"

"Hey, that's more experience than I have," Rick says. "Besides, I need you on this one."

What can I say? I've just found out this man has looked out for me since my first day of kindergarten. Even if he's breaking my heart, I owe him.

I close my eyes in defeat. "I'll be happy to stop by— just let me know when."

"Tomorrow," Rick says. "I'm on duty all day."

"I'll come before my classes then. Let's say eight-thirty."

Just then we hear the sounds of the parrots coming to roost for the night. I guess if parrots can figure out how to survive on the streets of Pasadena, I can figure out how to celebrate a lightbulb.

After we've eaten the salad, Rick leaves and I go back up to my room. The Sisterhood journal is sitting miles away on Marilee's desk, but I open the drawer in my nightstand and pull out a tablet of paper I use for school. I can write everything down here and then tape the page into the Sisterhood journal. It takes me a couple of minutes to start, but when I do, this is what I write.

My friend, Rick, has Girl Scout cookies that I sold him over a decade ago, before I even had cancer. It's weird to think that, if things had turned out differ-

ent, those cookies would have lived longer than me. It makes me wonder about life. How can some things go on and on while other things, that are much more important, die so young? How could a cookie live longer than me? It doesn't seem right.

At least I managed to keep Marilee's secret. I do sometimes talk without thinking when I'm around Rick, so that was good for me. The reason I sometimes talk too much around him is probably nerves.

Oh, I just realized something—maybe Marilee is having pre-wedding jitters. I love my brother, but I can see why someone might be nervous about marrying him. After all, he does have some annoying habits. Like the Old Mother Hen thing—he really is overly protective of those he loves. Maybe Marilee is wondering how she can live her life with someone hovering over her all of the time. If that's the case, I should have been more sensitive. If anyone knows how someone who's overprotective can drive another person nuts, it is me. I'll need to talk to Marilee. Really Quinn is a wonderful man, and it's not that hard to figure out how to deal with that one tiny flaw, but maybe she needs some pointers.

I go to bed early that night, and before I know it, I'm dreaming of chocolate-coated Girl Scout cookies—rows and rows of frozen cookies. And they all have the faces of Rick's old girlfriends. Even in my dream, I know it's not right that he used the cookies I sold him to impress other women.

It's too bad I'm too old to kick him in the shins.

Chapter Seven

"People see God every day, they just don't recognize him."

—Pearl Bailey

Rose brought this quote to us one hot summer evening. She asked each of us to name a person who had been kind to us during the previous week. We all remembered this one particular nurse's aide who had brought around cups of water in the doctor's office when we were waiting to get our blood drawn. None of us had thought to ask the woman her name, but we all regretted the oversight when we sat in our meeting later remembering her. Since then, I've tried to get the name of anyone who has been particularly kind to me.

I wake up to the sounds of the wild parrots the next morning. They're quiet at night, but they like to squawk at each other almost as soon as it's light outside. Which would be—I turn to look at my clock—seven-thirty. They're late this morning, probably because of the overcast skies. Their early and noisy rising is one reason the birds are not always welcome in the neighborhoods around here.

I love them, though. I've often wondered what the red-headed birds are saying out there and if they're complaining about the wetness of the overnight rain or the quality of the seeds they've been able to find that morning.

The birds should be happy with today at least. The sky is a little overcast, but there is no rain, and the sun will probably shine, even if somewhat feebly, until it sets tonight. I'm guessing this will be a fine day for birds.

It certainly is a welcome day for me. I take a moment to greet God since He is the one responsible for this glorious gray morning. I must admit I feel a little shy as I whisper some words to Him. I'm still learning about prayer, and although Pastor Engstrom gave me a couple of books to help explain it, I haven't read them yet. Praying to God is actually pretty amazing. It's even more astonishing than the thought that those birds are out in the trees communicating with each other.

After I say good-morning to God, I take a minute to ask Him to help Marilee work out whatever problem she has with Quinn. God already knows I want them to get back together, so I put it in His hands, figuring He knows how to make it happen.

By the time I'm ready to leave my bed, I need to hurry to make my meeting with Rick. I get dressed and grab the same gray cable sweater I wore yesterday; it's big enough to cover the white T-shirt I put on with my jeans. As I race through the kitchen, I grab an oatmeal breakfast bar and rip off its wrapper to take a bite. I have some of my Macy's makeup in my car, so I sit a minute in my mother's driveway and put on eye makeup and that Pink Passion lip gloss.

I drive to Old Town and park my car in the structure down the street from the fire station. I walk fast and am out of breath when I finally get to the building. It's chilly outside, and I keep my sweater pulled tight around me. I'm only five minutes late, though.

"There you are," Rick says as I open the side door and step into the station. It takes a few seconds for my eyes to adjust to the shadows in the main part of the building. There's a huge red fire engine that sits in the middle of this place, but I can see Rick standing on the other side near the large garage door. Behind him is a rack of yellow turnout coats, with their gray reflective stripes, that the firemen put on before they ride the truck out on a call. A row of shiny helmets sits neatly on a shelf above the rack. Most of the helmets are yellow, except for one that's orange for the captain.

As I walk closer, I see some more helmets dangling by cords from iron spikes higher up on the brick wall. These helmets are old, dented and scarred by what must have been fire.

"Those are our good-luck hats," Rick says as he follows my eyes to the beat-up helmets. "Each one of those helmets helped save the life of someone at the station. They go back for decades. I don't know what the oldest is—I think it's in the 1920s. We have a record somewhere."

Rick is silent for a moment, just looking at them.

"Some of the guys have a favorite helmet they always touch before they go out on a call. They call it extra protection."

"Well, I can see why—" I start to say.

"Quinn won't do it," Rick interrupts me. "He used to, before he became a Christian. But he says a man of faith doesn't need superstition when he has God to keep him safe."

"Well, maybe he doesn't need it, but—can't it just be a comforting habit?"

I am thinking of my Lizzie stone. I'm not so sure it's been a good-luck charm for me as much as it's been a way for me to think I have some control over my life. For years, it has been immensely comforting to have something I could do that I believed would help me. It took me through kindergarten and cancer. Of course, that was all before I gave my life to God. Now I'm supposed to ask Him for what I need. It's not quite the same as having something I can hold in my hand, but I am working on praying instead of doing what I used to do.

I need to get rid of the Lizzie stone, though. I put it in my sweater pocket this morning so that hopefully I can find the right place to leave it some time today. Once I find the place to leave it, I'll be able to let it go— I hope.

"I don't think touching those helmets can just be a habit," Rick says softly. "At least not in Quinn's book."

Neither one of us mentions that Quinn's book these days is the Bible. He reads it every chance he gets. Which makes him much more of an authority than me.

I stand there a minute and wonder if I'll ever get the

Christian life figured out. I relate more to those pagan people in the Old Testament with their idols and their fears than I do the faith-filled Christians in the New Testament. Not that they were perfect, either.

"I suppose it would be okay to touch the helmets just in an acknowledgment that they were involved in a life-and-death situation," Rick finally adds. "Out of respect maybe of what God has done."

My lips curve up as I look at him. "So my Lizzie stone could be a memorial to the fact that I survived kindergarten. Like that Old Testament guy who piled up rocks that time because God had saved him."

The man's name escapes me, and I don't think Rick knows it, either.

"Well, I'm sure God would want us to remember that He helped you get through kindergarten," Rick agrees with a flash of a grin. "As I recall, it was quite the struggle."

I nod. "I didn't want to stay there, but my mom said I had to learn how to color."

The morning light is filtering in through the row of high windows above the garage door that the fire engine uses to come in and out. I can hear the murmur of people in the upstairs area, but no one is down here with Rick and me. With all of the polished old wood, the place feels as historic as it is. So much drama has played out here over the years.

We are quiet for a minute, and then Rick says, "I'm sorry about kindergarten. I always thought you colored just fine."

"I didn't stay in the lines," I confess.

"I know." Rick lifts his hand up to touch my cheek.

I can almost sense a kiss coming.

Just then we both hear the sound of boots tromping down the back stairs.

Rick takes his hand away from my face, and I realize there won't be a kiss today, either.

"Hey, Kiefer," someone calls out. "Do you know where the other bag of coffee is? I can't stand that decaf stuff."

I see the outline of a guy walking toward us. He's big and tall and his features become clearer as he walks closer. I recognize the firemen that come into the Pews, but he is not one of them.

"It's in the left cupboard," Rick says curtly. "Top shelf. And that's not decaf in that red bag. It's vanilla something-or-the-other."

"Well, well," the other fireman says as he keeps walking closer. He's looking at me and smiling. "Coffee isn't the only thing that wakes me up in the morning. Do we have company here?"

"It's Quinn's sister," Rick says. And then adds with emphasis, "His *little* sister."

"She doesn't look so little to me," the fireman says as he gives me a wink. "Any time you want someone to show you around the station here, just ask for me, Jake Nelson. I can answer any questions and—"

"I can show her around," Rick says a little abruptly.

I know Rick can show me everything. Still, it's nice to have someone acknowledge that I'm an adult, so I smile at the man politely. "Thanks for offering, though."

"No problem," the fireman says as he turns to go. "When you get tired of Kiefer here, you just let me know."

Well, there's not much to say to that, I think to myself as the man walks away. Apparently, though, Rick has a different opinion. He barely waits for the footsteps on the stairs to end before he begins.

"You absolutely don't want to encourage Jake there," Rick says. "He doesn't know how to have a committed relationship. He bounces from one woman to the next like he's in a ping-pong tournament."

It's Quinn and the math geeks all over again. No man will ever be steady enough for me to date.

"He probably doesn't mean any harm," I say.

"Yeah, well," Rick says, and he doesn't look too happy.

I'm not so happy myself. I don't need two Mother Hens in my life.

"I should really get going," I say. "Speaking of coffee reminds me I haven't had any this morning. I think I'll go by the Pews and get a cup before I head off to classes."

Rick nods. "You've probably seen enough to start thinking about how we can pull off the celebration anyway."

"Sure," I say as I start walking to the door.

"I'll be in touch," Rick says as I open the door.

I turn and wave.

It's still overcast when I step out of the fire station. I give a quick glance to the modern fire station they built next to this one. That one is clearly the station they use for the serious work. I'll have to explore the inside areas there someday soon, as that may be the more sensible place for the main part of the celebration.

I don't want to take the time to do it now, though. I really am hoping a cup of Uncle Lou's coffee will make me feel better about the day.

It starts to drizzle before I get to the Pews, and I run the last few yards. My hair has a tendency to get frizzy in the damp, and I still have to go to my classes, so I don't want to look too bad.

The air is warm inside the Pews, and I smell coffee. There are only a few tables with people at them, so I walk up to the counter. I see Carly walk out of the kitchen with a white dishcloth tied around her jeans and a coffee pot in her hand.

"I didn't know you were working today," I say as I sit down at one of the stools at the counter.

"Shelley called in sick," Carly says as she pulls a cup off the tray behind the counter and sets it in front of me.

"Coffee?"

I nod. "I need to wake up before class."

I watch as Carly pours me a cup of hot liquid.

"I don't suppose you've seen Marilee," I say after I've taken my first sip.

Carly shakes her head. "She must still be sick. I haven't seen her come in this morning."

I know from my experience yesterday that just because Marilee isn't making her presence known, it doesn't mean she's not here. I wait until Carly goes back into the kitchen and then I walk down the hall to Marilee's office. I knock at the door, and this time, the door opens a little. The light is off in the room, and it doesn't seem like anyone is there, but something has happened. There are baseball caps everywhere. It looks like someone took them off their neatly stacked rack and threw them all over the room.

I open the door completely just to be sure nothing else is wrong. I know Marilee never keeps any money in the office, so there would be no reason for anyone to try and rob the place.

When I have the door open, I see that it couldn't have been a robbery. The baseball caps are tossed in every direction, but none of the papers look like they've been pulled out of the file cabinets. The only thing on the desk surface is the Sisterhood journal, which is lying open. Apparently, Marilee didn't take it home with her after all.

I start picking up the caps. Knowing Marilee, she will be upset if she sees them tossed around like this. I notice her Dodgers cap isn't with the others; it was her favorite because her dad actually took her to one of their games when he gave it to her. Her parents are divorced, and she and her father had a hard time of it for years. She always thought half of the reason her father left her and her mother was because of her cancer. Marilee and her father are doing fine now, though.

I stack the caps on the desk and pick up the Sisterhood journal. I see that Marilee has written something.

It's not fair. It's not fair. It's not fair. I can't go through it again. Please, don't make me go through it again.

That's all, but it makes my blood turn to ice. I clasp the journal to me and run to find Carly.

"What's wrong?" Carly sees me coming down the hall before I even get to the main part of the diner.

"We've got to go find Marilee," I say.

Just then Uncle Lou comes out of the kitchen, too. He's works the grill most mornings.

"What's wrong?" he says when he sees my face.

"I think something's wrong with Marilee," I say. That's as much as I can say. "We need to go find her."

"She didn't come in," he says. "I thought she was home sick."

"Is her mother there?" I ask.

Uncle Lou shakes his head and then looks at Carly. "I can cover for a bit. You go with Lizabett."

Carly and I don't talk as we half run to her car. She is parked closer than I am since Uncle Lou has a few places in the back alley for his employees to use.

While Carly starts her car, I read her the words Marilee wrote.

"She said yesterday she couldn't get married," I confess. "But I thought she was just mad at Quinn for some reason. I didn't think she might be worried about—"

I let my voice trail off. I don't want to say the word. But with Carly there's no need. She understands. Her knuckles are white as she grips the steering wheel and pulls out of the alley.

"Surely she would tell us," Carly mutters as she turns onto Union Street. "I don't think she's due for her mammogram or anything. She always tells us when she's going in to get one."

It takes us ten long minutes to drive to the house where Marilee lives with her mother. The Spanish-style house looks quiet when we pull into the driveway. Marilee's car is there, though.

There's a white fence around the house's yard, and we walk over to the front gate. There's a bougainvillea vine that wraps around the curved overhang jutting out over the small porch.

Carly and I barely step onto the porch before I have my fist up knocking at the door.

"Marilee," I call as I'm knocking.

For a moment, I think she's not home, and then I hear someone opening the door.

I see more of the blue Dodger baseball cap than I do of Marilee's face. She's standing there in the crack of an open door, looking forlorn.

"I'm sick," she says.

"That's why we're here," I say softly. "In case you need help."

Marilee is silent for a long minute. "I don't want to talk about it."

"You don't need to talk," Carly says. "We'll just sit with you a bit."

Marilee opens the door wider and stands there in her robe. I can see her trembling. At first, her head is down, but then she looks up so she can see us.

"I found a lump," she finally whispers.

Carly and I both step closer to Marilee and wrap her in a hug. We all just stand there for a while until Marilee stops shaking.

"Have you made an appointment with your doctor?" Carly asks.

Marilee shakes her head. "I can't bring myself to call. It makes it seem so real."

"It might be all right," I say as I press her closer again. "Not all lumps are cancer."

"But with my history," Marilee says and then swallows. "I thought that was all behind me. I was going to get married and have a normal life." She stops and looks at me. "You didn't tell Quinn, did you? I'm not ready to talk to him yet."

I smile a little. "If I had told Quinn, he would already be here. He thinks you have a cold."

"Good," Marilee says. "I don't want to tell him until—"

I hate to see her looking so torn up.

"My dad—" Marilee swallows. "I know he said it wasn't the cancer, but—"

"Quinn's not afraid of cancer," I say. "He'd never leave you because—"

"But maybe he should," Marilee says. "It's too hard."

"We don't even know you have cancer again," Carly says firmly. "The first thing we need to do is get you an appointment with the doctor. Everything else can wait."

The three of us go inside Marilee's house and sit down at the table in the dining room. Marilee has a small Rolodex sitting on a stand in the corner of the room and Carly brings it over so we can find the number for her doctor.

"We need to call Becca, too," I say as Carly dials the doctor's number.

After the calls are made, we just sit around the table. I notice that Marilee keeps her cap pulled close over her face and that I have, without thinking, already pulled my Lizzie stone out of my sweater pocket and started rubbing it. We stay there for a while.

"I'm not sure I can go through it all again," Marilee finally says.

"You won't be alone," I say.

"We've done it before, we can do it again," Carly declares.

It all sounds hollow, though, even to my ears. God was supposed to have cured us. I know we weren't Christians when we first got our clean bill of health from the disease, but we've done our time. How could He let this happen again?

Marilee is right. It's not fair.

I look down at the stone in my hand. I hadn't meant to start using it again, but I have.

Chapter Eight

"In feature films the director is God; in documentary films God is the director."

—Alfred Hitchcock

I brought this quote to the Sisterhood meeting, because I thought it was funny. We'd had the earlier Hitchcock quotes, and so I'd read a book about the man. He claimed the reason he could write scary movies was because he was a coward. A brave man, he said, would never dream up things terrifying enough to make audiences scream. The sisters all decided we liked Hitchcock better because he had been scared like we were.

Marilee agreed to get dressed and come back to the Sisterhood room with us. Becca said she'd skip her classes and meet us there.

I didn't realize until then that I was cutting my classes, too. Not that I had any intention of going now.

Fifteen minutes later, I could feel the worry rising up inside me as we walked into the doors of the Pews. It suddenly occurred to me that Hitchcock had never made a movie where the terrifying thing was illness. In life, though, that's where most people's fears centered.

It had been a long time since I felt this kind of urgency when the Sisterhood came together. The problems we face now are about our careers, or our classes, or—for those that have them—our boyfriends. I know none of us have forgotten the days when we were scared for our lives, though. That's a much more primitive, breathless fear.

Becca is already in the Sisterhood room when the three of us walk inside. She stands up and walks toward us. We all come together just inside the French doors and, within two seconds, wrap ourselves in a tight group hug. Then we sit down. Usually we spread out at the table, but today we are huddled next to each other. We all want to be within touching distance of Marilee.

"When did you feel the lump?" Becca asks. She is the one who takes charge in emergencies. When we first started meeting, it took me a while to get used to that, but now I am grateful. I want someone to fix everything.

"I noticed it Sunday morning in the shower," Marilee says. "I usually do a quick breast exam and—"

Marilee stops and swallows.

"We made a doctor's appointment for tomorrow morning." Carly takes up the flow of information. "That was the soonest he could see her."

"We'll know more then," Becca says, frowning like she is planning a military campaign and needs to line up all of the details. I guess that's what she's doing.

"You'll need someone to go to the appointment with you," Becca announces. "What time is it?"

"Oh, I don't need—" Marilee says, but her voice is halfhearted. "Everyone's so busy."

"Don't be silly," Carly says. "We can all go if you want."

"Absolutely," Becca says as I nod my agreement.

"Well, I don't need everybody." Marilee gives us a slight smile. "The doctor's office doesn't have that much waiting room. But maybe—" Marilee looks at me. "Could you come with me?"

"Of course." I try not to let my surprise show. I'm usually not the one in the Sisterhood that the others turn to when they have problems.

I look around, and I'm further amazed that neither Becca nor Carly seems to be shocked by Marilee's choice. Maybe I am more grown-up in their eyes than I ever suspected.

Just then there's a knock on the French doors. Uncle Lou enters with a tray of hot tea and some buttered toast. He has included a little dish of that imported raspberry jam Marilee loves. Usually, her eyes light up when she sees that stuff. Today I'm not sure she even notices it's there.

"I thought you could use—" he begins, and then he sees Marilee's face. "Are you okay?"

We're silent as Marilee stands and then walks over to her uncle. He's a big teddy bear of a man with a balding head and a white dishtowel wrapped around his waist for an apron. Uncle Lou sets the tray down on the far side of the table and enfolds his niece in a hug.

"I will be okay," Marilee says quietly to him. "I just found a little lump, that's all."

Uncle Lou hugs her even tighter. "Have you told your mom?"

Marilee shakes her head. "But I will. Tonight."

"And your dad?" Uncle Lou asks.

"Soon. I'll tell him soon."

I'm glad Marilee is telling people what is wrong. One thing we all learned is that there's nothing worse than holding a secret like that inside oneself. She needs to tell Quinn, too, but I don't say anything about it right now. She has a few hours before he will start to worry in earnest anyway.

After we've had our hugs and our tea, the sisters sit quietly around the table. We're all feeling a little bit spent. Marilee has said she doesn't want to talk about it any more, and, truthfully, there's not much more to say until we talk to the doctor.

"Tell me about your date with Rick," Marilee says suddenly. Her eyes perk up at the question. "Did he kiss you?"

I don't have the heart to tell her the kiss landed square on my forehead. I try to think of something else I can tell her that she'll like.

"He wore a suit, and he looked as classy as Cary Grant does in those old movies," I offer. That doesn't seem like enough, so I add, "And he did say he's not opposed to getting married."

"Really?" Marilee says, brightening up even more.

"You go, girl," Becca adds while Carly just beams at me.

"Well, he was telling that more to the waiter than to me," I feel compelled to add. "But Alfred thought I'd make a good wife."

I see everyone's blank looks.

"Alfred was our waiter."

"Ah," Marilee says with a sigh. "That's so romantic—when even the waiter can tell there's some connection."

I figure I better stop while I'm ahead. There's nothing more about the evening that will make her continue smiling anyway. Except maybe— "Oh, and Rick offered to help with your wedding. Not that we'll need—" Oops. I forgot. "I'm sorry. I didn't mean to remind you."

Marilee has a tear in her eye now. "I don't know how to tell Quinn. He's gone through so much in his life already with your dad dying when he was so young and then your cancer and—well, even if he's willing to stay, I don't want him to have to go through the worry about me, too."

"Of course, he's willing to stay," I say. "Besides, there's no way to spare Quinn. He loves you and he'll worry even if all you have is a hangnail. It's just the way he's made."

Marilee has a small smile now. "He is a sweetheart."

We all sit in silence some more. Finally, Marilee decides she might as well go straighten up her office, so she stands. We all get up and Becca says she's going back to her classes. Carly doesn't have to go far to get back to work, but we all know that the lunch hour will be starting soon at the Pews and Uncle Lou will need her help.

I walk with Marilee down the hall to her office.

"I sort of already picked up the caps." I pause. "And the Sisterhood journal was open, so I took it, too."

I have the journal in the book bag I have on my arm.

Marilee nods. "That's how you knew then—the journal."

I nod and suddenly realize that I still have my fingers closed over the stone in my sweater pocket. I relax and draw my hand out of my pocket.

Marilee has noticed, though. "The Lizzie stone?"

By this time, we're at her office door. She pushes it open.

"I've tried to stop, but it's not easy," I confess to Marilee as we both sit down, her in the chair behind the desk and me in the side chair.

"I know what you mean," Marilee says as she takes the baseball cap off her head. "I have the same problem. I get panicked and I want the kind of comfort I had before, so—" she gestures around the room "—I go for my caps."

I swallow. "Rick thinks it might be superstitious—me and my rock."

"He's probably right," Marilee says with a twist to her lips. "It's the same with me. The only difference is that Rick gave you the stone and my dad gave me the baseball caps. And I think it's the fact that they gave us those things that makes them so powerful and so hard to give up."

I think on that for a moment. "You mean, maybe it's not the Lizzie stone itself that I keep turning to?"

Marilee nods. "I wonder if it's Rick you trust and not that piece of rock."

I don't know about that. I could ask Rick to do something for me if that's what I wanted. But then—maybe the Rick I trust is the boy he used to be. Rick hasn't changed that much over the years, but I did idolize that boy as only a five-year-old girl could.

"Well, think about it," Marilee continues. "All I know

is that the caps, for me, have more to do with my dad than they do with my love of baseball."

"Your dad gave you some great caps…." My voice trails off. I'm not really comfortable thinking that all of these years I've wanted Rick to ease my worries. I'd much rather just be relying on that old piece of rock.

"Anyway, the important thing is that we should be turning to God for help instead of anything else," Marilee says wearily. "I know that in my head, but what did I do when I got scared? I ran right back to what I believed before I became a Christian. I'm one of God's children, but I keep wandering around in the wilderness. At least you only became a Christian a few days ago. I should know better."

We sit together for a few minutes.

"We could always pray now," I finally say. I don't know what else to offer her for comfort. "God's still here, and He knows we're scared."

We hold hands, and I pray for my friend. "Dear Father, we need Your help. We don't even know how to trust You like we should. Please help Marilee and give the doctor insight when we go to see him. May she be free of cancer. Meanwhile, give us all peace. May we be blessed in Jesus's name. Amen."

After I finish the prayer, we sit some more.

"I might still wait until after I talk to the doctor before I say anything to Quinn," Marilee finally says. "I won't really know anything to tell him until then anyway."

"You know you're worried," I say. "He'd want to know that."

Marilee doesn't say anything.

"I won't say anything to him, though," I finally say. "It's your decision on when you tell him."

I figure I might as well learn how to be a good sister-in-law now. I don't want to be between her and my brother later.

"Thank you," Marilee says.

Speaking of being a good sister-in-law, I can't help but ask, "You are still going to marry him, though, aren't you?"

Marilee looks at me, and I see the tiredness in her eyes. "Tell me again about the plans you have for the wedding. Okay?"

I know that's a pretty evasive answer, but I'm not going to press her for any more.

"I've got calls in for some outdoor places to have it," I say. I have the details written down at home, but I know the general picture by heart. "There's Descanso Gardens. They'll let us have a small wedding if we wait for the weather to warm up. I've got a good one-time discount with them because of school. It would be beautiful, and we could save on flowers because there are so many nice ones growing in the ground there already. They even have a nice white gazebo we can use in the ceremony."

With the discount, we can barely afford their fees, but it is my first choice as a location.

"A gazebo would be nice," Marilee says with her eyes half-closed. She's starting to get a beautiful expression on her face, and I know she's picturing herself saying her vows to my brother amidst all the trees and flowers of the garden. The smell of the rose bushes alone adds romance to the setting.

"There aren't many indoor places we can afford," I

continue. "But the wedding chapel on Hill Avenue has some dates open in a couple of months. We might get a discount, too, if we do it on a Thursday night."

One of my classmates got an excellent deal from them. It's still a little out of our price range, but we might be able to cut some corners and make it work.

"The Sisterhood meets on Thursdays," Marilee says.

"We can miss one time for your wedding," I say.

I don't tell Marilee, but the cost of any of the other nice locations is more than we can afford even if we skimp on everything else.

"I've called the man who owns the horse and buggy you see around Old Town sometimes." I forget about the location and keep on painting the picture. "I thought we might get him to drive you and Quinn away from the place after you get married. You know, with one of those 'Just Married' signs on the back. That always looks so romantic. He said he even has some floral arrangements he can put around the buggy. Pink roses, I think."

I don't mention that they are plastic floral arrangements. And that, in exchange for a huge discount, I've had to promise to do my best to use him for three future weddings. He's a nice guy, though, and will work with us.

"Quinn said that a couple of the guys at the station have daughters young enough to be flower girls," I add.

"Really?" Marilee's eyes brighten. "I've always wanted flower girls."

"I'll have him ask them, then."

We're silent for a minute.

Then Marilee says softly, "I'll be able to spend more time helping you in a few days. We'll need music, too.

Maybe some old-fashioned love songs. Or someone playing a violin. I always think that's so romantic."

"Of course," I say as I add a violinist to my list. I wonder if I should put a note up on the student bulletin board at PCC. Which just leaves the other things. "And we'll need to talk about the bridesmaid dresses. And renting the tuxedos for the men."

Marilee sighs. "Quinn will look so handsome in a tuxedo."

I nod, hoping she's right. Handsome has never been a word I've used to describe my brother. He's steady; he's loyal; he fights like a tiger to protect anyone he loves—but handsome? Not to me, but I'm glad Marilee thinks so. Of course, my taste goes more toward tall men with thick black hair and laughing eyes.

Just then Carly knocks at the door and asks if we'd like some salads for lunch. That brings both of us back to reality.

"Oh." Marilee looks at me. "I forgot you have class today."

"I can miss it," I say.

"Not if you're taking off tomorrow when we go to the doctor," Marilee says. "You need to be learning all you can so you'll know how to make my wedding spectacular."

Well, how can I resist that? Besides, she's got a point. I'm counting on the perks I get in my classes to pull this wedding off. Maybe I can stay afterward today and ask one of my instructors for some suggestions. There's got to be a way to make wedding dreams come true on a very small budget.

I eat my turkey cobb salad and then walk back down Colorado toward the parking structure. I hesitate outside of the old fire station before deciding to step inside again just to see if I get any more inspiration for the celebration there.

The fire station feels like a cathedral when I go inside. It must be the high ceilings and the way the light from the windows hits the original wood on the walls. What looks like mahogany covers the walls of the main room, where the fire truck is usually parked. I don't know where the truck is, but I think it might be next door getting washed. As I understand it, the fire engine in this building is a spare one anyway. The main action these days takes place in the newer building next door.

That's probably why I don't hear anyone around. They might all be out back doing drills, too.

I walk over to the brass pole that goes up through a hole in the ceiling to the living quarters on the second floor. Not very many guys use that space now since most of them bunk next door. I look up through the hole, and, at the very top of the ceiling way up high, I see the old lightbulb burning away in the shadows. It doesn't give off much light at all, but then it's only a four-watt bulb—which is bigger than a Christmas-tree light but not nearly as powerful as most lightbulbs are today. Even in the pitch black of night I don't think that old bulb would give off enough light to read by. But it would certainly help firefighters get their gear on.

I need to get to class. As I drive over to the college, I try to think of ideas for both events. Working on my plans keeps my fears for Marilee in the background. I take a few minutes to talk with my instructor after class, and he gives me fliers for more vendors that give student discounts.

When I finish there, I start the drive home. My plan

is to get home before Quinn and be in my room reading when he drives up, just in case he has questions about Marilee. I don't want to betray my friend's trust, but I don't want to have to evade any of Quinn's questions, either. If I can just get through tonight, everything will be better. I believe and hope Marilee will tell my brother everything after we go to the doctor tomorrow.

I park my car on the street and lock it up for the night.

I'm almost up the brick walk to my mom's front door when I see a long tube lying on the porch. I have to get close to it before I realize it's a single rose, wrapped in a tube of hard plastic.

I pick up the tube and a note falls to the porch.

"Lizabett—Sorry we got interrupted. Rick." That's all the note says. I turn the tube upside down hoping something else will fall out to explain, but nothing does. When Rick said interrupted, did he mean when we got interrupted looking at the fire station or was he thinking we got interrupted when he was going to *finally* kiss me?

I shake my head. No wonder I'm going crazy. I don't understand men at all. A woman would have made that note a whole lot more specific. I open the door and walk inside.

The rose is a lovely pink one, and I put it in one of my mom's crystal vases so I can take it up to my room. That way I will be able to admire it from my bed and it won't arouse any curiosity in my brother if he stops by to see Mom tonight.

My brother is going to be so upset with me when he realizes I kept Marilee's news from him. And, truthfully, I won't blame him. He's a lot stronger than Marilee thinks. He can handle her news. What he might not be able to handle, though, is her not telling him about it. I'm not quite sure how I would feel about that if I were him, either.

A couple of hours later, I hear Quinn downstairs talking to Mom. He doesn't stay long. I listen, but I don't hear Rick's voice at all. I go to sleep looking at the way the rose looks in the moonlight shining through the window. I can't believe Rick sent me a rose.

Chapter Nine

❧

"People are like stained-glass windows. They
sparkle and shine when the sun is out, but when
the darkness sets in, their true beauty is revealed
only if there is a light from within."

—Elizabeth Kubler Ross

*When we were having our battles with chemo, Carly
brought this quote to one of our meetings. Along
with it, she brought a book with beautiful pictures
of stained-glass windows in old European cathedrals.
I don't think I ever appreciated the beauty of a
church before that. The deep reds and purples were
awe-inspiring. I wondered if God could really be
inside a place like that. Rose mentioned that the
pictures reminded her of some of the churches in the
older sections of Los Angeles.*

*In the next few weeks, each of us went to visit a
church that had big stained-glass windows. I went to
the Episcopal church high up on Lake Avenue in*

Pasadena. It was the first time I sensed that there might be a God and that He just might be more magnificent than I had ever thought. No wonder people back in ancient times made such a big deal about those windows.

The pink rose is even more beautiful in the thin light of dawn. I hear the wild parrots outside having their usual conversation with each other. I could lie in bed for hours with this kind of peace. Of course, all I would be doing would be hiding from the problems of the day. I don't lie there much longer; Marilee's appointment is at nine o'clock, and I have to get dressed and down to the Pews. I need to be strong for Marilee, so I do not think about what might be happening.

I am planning to drive Marilee to the doctor's, so Uncle Lou said I could park in one of the spaces behind the diner when I pick her up. After I pull into the space, I get out of my car. It's early enough that, even in the alley, I smell bacon frying along with fresh cinnamon rolls baking. Uncle Lou puts out a traditional breakfast. Marilee has persuaded him to compromise and go a little trendy with the lunch and dinner menus, but he prides himself on serving a working man's breakfast.

When I open the door to the Pews, I see that Marilee is sitting at the counter. She looks up and motions for me to come over.

"Uncle Lou insists I eat breakfast. I hope you don't mind," she says.

"Of course not," I say as I walk over and sit on the stool next to her.

I look at her and she looks at me and we hug tightly. I wipe away a few tears.

"I might have something to eat, too," I finally say.

"I'm sure Uncle Lou will be happy if you do," Marilee says. "You know how he is about breakfast."

Uncle Lou comes out of the kitchen with a pot of coffee and pours me a cup. "Marilee's having my ham omelet. What can I get for you? You still like the vegetable one with all of the onions and peppers?"

I nod. "Please. And wheat toast, no butter."

"You got it," Uncle Lou says as he walks back into the kitchen.

"I should just have dry toast, too," Marilee mutters when her uncle is gone. "It's healthier and—"

"Nonsense," I say. "If you want some butter and that raspberry jam, you should have it."

"Yeah, I suppose it won't make much difference at this point," she says.

"We're not at 'this point' yet," I say bracingly. "Everybody gets panicked when they find a lump—and you do need to check it out—but it could be anything."

"I just have a bad feeling," Marilee says as she twists the paper napkin that was wrapped around her silverware.

"Well, I have a good feeling," I say as I look Marilee squarely in the eyes. I might be exaggerating, but I'm working hard to keep my worry down. "It doesn't need to be what you're thinking."

Marilee studies my eyes for a minute. "Thank you."

Uncle Lou brings us each a glass of orange juice with our omelets.

We bow, and I quietly pray, "Father, please be with

us today. We thank You for meeting our needs already, and we ask Your protection. Please, Father, don't let Marilee have cancer. Amen."

I look up and am surprised. When we bowed our heads, Marilee and I had the counter to ourselves, but now there's a fireman sitting just two stools down from me. It's the guy, Jake, that I met only yesterday.

"Oh, hello," I say when I see he's looking at me.

Jake nods and smiles. "Sorry to hear about your friend."

"Oh, I—please don't say anything about what you heard," I say. "We don't want anyone to know."

"My lips are sealed," Jake says and turns to look at his menu.

"It's just that not everyone understands," I continue on even though I know I should stop.

This gets his attention again, and he looks up with a frown. "I hope you're not talking about Kiefer. He's a fireman. We pride ourselves in being able to handle any situation."

"No, no, I just—well, if you could just forget what you heard. That would be the best," I continue to the finish line even though I know I should never have started this conversation.

Jake nods politely and then looks away when Uncle Lou finally comes out from the kitchen and asks for the man's order.

"Sorry about that," I whisper to Marilee.

"It's okay," Marilee says. "Let's just eat and get going, though. I don't like all this secrecy."

I nod miserably. I don't like it, either.

We get to the doctor's office an hour later. Marilee wants to see him alone, so I sit in the waiting room flipping through a few magazines without reading them. I have the journal in my purse, but I am too keyed up to write anything. I started to write something, but all I got down was

Please, please, please, no cancer for Marilee. Not now. Not ever. Not again. Please, please, please. Help us, Father.

I can't just keep pleading like that, so I close the journal and put it back in my purse. Now I'm sitting here trying to look calm.

"Would you like something to drink?" the receptionist says to me from where she's sitting behind a counter. "I could get you some coffee or tea."

I start to refuse, but then say, "Thanks, I could use some water. I'm Lizabett. What's your name?"

"Anna," the woman says with a smile as she stands up. "Anna Baxter."

I stand, too. "I can get the water if you just point me in the right direction."

Anna and I talk for few more minutes, and I sit back down with my water. It helps to have a friendly face in a waiting room like this.

It seems like forever, but Marilee finally comes out of the back part of the office.

I wait until we get in the car before I ask my questions. "How'd it go?"

Marilee shrugs. "He could feel the lump, but he didn't know what it was. It could just be a cyst. He's scheduling me for a mammogram and a needle biopsy. I'll know more after that. He's doing the mammogram this Friday and the biopsy next Wednesday."

I nod. "I don't have any classes on Friday if you want—"

"Oh, I definitely want your company," Marilee says with a tight smile. "You're good at this."

"I am?" I'm shocked.

Marilee nods. "You know when to hold someone's hands and when to give them some space. Lots of people can do one or the other, but it takes a special person to know when to do which."

That makes me feel good, especially after my indiscreet words this morning in front of that fireman. Which reminds me.

"You *are* going to tell Quinn, though, aren't you?" I ask as I start my car. "He might not be the kind that gives you much space, but I can't keep avoiding him and I'm afraid he's going to guess something is wrong just by looking at my face."

"Well, surely he can't tell—"

"You know Quinn. He can tell."

Marilee laughs. "I guess you're right. He has instincts about things."

"With my face, I'm not sure if he has instincts or he just knows me. I've never been able to hide things from him."

I drive back to the Pews. The parking space behind the alley is still open, so I pull in there.

"Come in for lunch," Marilee says. "You've got time before your one o'clock class."

I walk into the diner with Marilee. The place is beginning to fill up, but I don't even need to look all of the way around before I see Quinn and Rick sitting at a table to the side.

"Uh-oh," I say softly to Marilee as I see Quinn stand up. "I think we've been busted."

I know Marilee doesn't want to tell Quinn she has the lump, but she's not going to have much choice when they're face-to-face. Now that I'm getting over the surprise of seeing him sitting there, I decide that it's a good thing. They need to talk.

I step away from Marilee, and she's looking so intently at my brother, I don't think she even notices. I look over at where Rick is sitting. Ordinarily, I wouldn't just walk over and sit at the table with him, but I'm feeling a little battle weary. There's a plate with a half-eaten sandwich where Quinn was sitting. I move it. Out of the corner of my eye, I see Marilee and Quinn walking down the hall to her office. That must mean she's going to tell him.

"Is she okay?" Rick asks as I sit down so I'm facing him.

"I don't know," I say. Then it hits me. "How did you guys know something was wrong?"

Rick winced. "Jake Nelson came in to the station, asking which one of us was the insensitive fool who couldn't understand that someone with cancer needs our support."

"He said he wouldn't tell," I protest indignantly.

"Yeah, well, he lied. People do that sometimes."

I know that, but I still don't think it's very nice.

"He could have told me that he was going to run right over and tell you both everything he heard," I finally say.

Rick shrugs. "He probably didn't want you to get mad at him."

I'm silent at that. It is true that I would have scolded him. Of course, he would have had it coming.

Finally, Rick starts to speak again quietly. "I've never seen Quinn like this. You and your friends can't keep things like this from him."

"I didn't want to," I admit. "But it wasn't my place to tell him. It had to come from Marilee."

Rick is silent for a bit. "I suppose that's right. But you wouldn't keep it a secret, would you? Not if you were the one who had the problem?"

Rick's eyes look vulnerable. He doesn't even bother to hide the fact, he just looks straight at me with all of the worry he's got churning inside of him.

"I thought it might be you," he adds softly. "Jake sometimes gets things mixed up."

I blink. Rick might not see me as the woman of his dreams, but he does see me as a dear friend. "No, I'm fine. Really."

"Good."

Rick and I just sit for a while after that. The waitress comes by, and I order a grilled tuna sandwich. Rick has a half-eaten roast-beef sandwich on his plate already.

"You know Quinn's going to want to move up the wedding date," Rick finally says. "He must have said that a dozen times while we were sitting here. He's worried he'll be left out if he doesn't get legally wed to Marilee soon. She might want to move it up, too."

"No one's set a wedding date," I say. "I suppose Quinn will insist on the pastor's study again."

I hate to let the fairytale wedding go.

"I don't think he's so set on the pastor's study as much as he is anxious to have it all happen right away," Rick says. "Maybe if you told him what you have that would work during the next month or so—"

"No place has openings that soon," I say. Especially none that honor the coupons I have from my courses. And anything else would be beyond what any of us can afford.

Rick looks at me. "So you're saying we have like—what—no options?"

"I'm working on it," I say a little defensively.

"I know you've been working on it," Rick adds softly. "There's never been any question of that. I saw all of your fliers. But this isn't going to be a normal timeline. Everyone will have to pitch in. I can make some calls for you, if you want. You can't do this by yourself."

I open my mouth and then close it. I remember what Marilee said about me relying on Rick as much as the Lizzie stone to rescue me. I don't want to do that.

"I should be fine. I have contacts from school and coupons with discounts."

Besides, I need to start relying on the God of the universe when I have worries. He can help me do what I need to do for Quinn and Marilee.

Rick is silent for a minute. "Well, if you need help, you know who to ask."

I nod. "Thanks. I appreciate that."

My sandwich arrives, and I'm glad for the distraction. Just then Marilee and Quinn start coming back down the hall. He has his arm around her, and I can see, even from here, that she has his ring back on her finger.

Rick must have been watching them, too, because he says, "Now, isn't that nice?"

Quinn and Rick need to go back to work, but I sit with Marilee for a while and finish my sandwich. She gets a cup of tomato basil soup.

"Rick seemed to think you two might want to get married soon," I say as she takes a spoonful of soup.

Marilee nods her head. "We decided we would."

I steel myself inwardly. I can do this. "Do you have a date set?"

"We figured next Saturday, March thirty-first," Marilee says. "But don't worry. We know we need to make changes. We won't have hordes of guests coming. We decided to trim the invitation list—just our immediate families, close friends and some of the people we work with. About sixty people in all."

Well, that rules out the pastor's study, I think to myself. That room can't accommodate nearly that many people. Which means we won't even have a backup location. I take a deep breath. I have no option but to go forward now.

"We should be sending out invitations already," I say. "Maybe we can just give people save-the-date invitations for now and set up a Web site so they can log on for the location later. That can be fun. We'll add some photos, too."

"I'm sorry," Marilee says as she smiles wanly. She looks so very tired. "We know there's not time to do the wedding like we planned. All we really need is a place that's big enough for people to sit. It won't be anything fancy. I figure I'll wear that beige suit of my mother's, and I won't need any bridesmaids. Quinn said maybe on our five-year anniversary we can do all of the things we wanted to do for our wedding."

But that will never be their *real* wedding. I keep my mouth shut, however. Marilee has enough to worry about. And it's the wedding planner's job to pull together the impossible.

"You're sure?" I finally ask gently. "You've always wanted a big, fancy wedding."

"All I want right now is to be married to Quinn," Marilee says.

"We should still try to find a dress for you. And maybe you could have at least one bridesmaid? And someone to sing? Not to mention flowers and photography."

Marilee smiles tightly. "I don't see how we'd pull it together. There's no time. It's only a week and a half away. And if we don't do the other things, having a fancy dress will only seem strange."

"But are you okay with not having any of those things?" I watch her closely. "You used to describe your wedding in such detail. You always wanted it all—the cake and the music and the flowers."

Marilee hesitates, but then she says softly, "I don't have the energy to pull it all together right now. Not with going to the doctor's and everything. And it's not fair to ask you to do it all. Even a wedding planner expects to work with the bride on most of it."

I can tell by the slight smile on her face that Marilee is already dreaming about my brother. She's certainly not dwelling on getting married in her mother's old suit. She's forgotten all about the lump in her breast and the fears in her heart. She's skipping past the wedding to the marriage.

Watching her face, I feel such a mixture of emotions. I am so glad she's found someone she loves and wants to marry, but at the same time I'm a little worried. And this is a worry that's not likely to go away. Marilee and Quinn are hopefully going to be married for a long time. Together they will go to the weddings of lots of their friends. Someday, God willing, they will even come to my wedding.

How is Marilee going to feel when she sees the elegant weddings of her friends? She has always dreamed of wearing a veil and eating wedding cake. She has talked of candlelight and roses—and all of the other things that make up a traditional wedding—for as long as I have known her.

I saw how the thought of her fairytale wedding could pull Marilee out of her pain. It's not fair that she can't have a wedding like that, not when she might be going back into that pain.

All of a sudden, I make my decision. I don't care about deadlines and impossible tasks. I am going to give Marilee her fairytale wedding. I don't know how, but I will. I owe that to her and my brother. Besides, I am the wedding planner and it's my job to make their dreams come true whether they have time to help or not.

Chapter Ten

"Good communication is as stimulating as black coffee, and just as hard to sleep after."
> —Anne Morrow Lindbergh

Uncle Lou gave us this quote for one of our meetings. He knew that we shared quotes and talked about them, so one night, when he brought us his usual pot of tea, he handed us this one printed on a napkin he'd received from his coffee supplier. We laughed a little and then compared our sleep habits. We decided Anne Morrow Lindbergh was wrong. At least for us, we slept better after we'd had a good conversation with each other. When we shared our troubles, we lost some of our anxiety and were able to relax enough to sleep.

It's eight o'clock when I drive home from my class, and I think to myself that there's no escaping Quinn tonight. I'm not surprised he's waiting on the porch, talking to Rick. It's dark already, but the porch light is doing its duty and I can see the two of them just fine as they sit there in the lawn chairs.

"You okay?" I ask Quinn as I walk up the steps.

He nods. "Don't ever keep that kind of news from me again, though."

His voice is strained and grim.

"I'd have to do the same thing again," I say quietly as I sit down on the top step and stretch out my legs. "Marilee has to tell you if something's wrong. You can't start your marriage with me in the middle."

"But—" Quinn starts, and then he stops and runs his hand over his head. "I guess you're right. I just always want to know when something's wrong."

"I can understand that."

I hear a rustle in the nearby tree and look up. I don't see anything. "The wild parrots?"

"They're already settled in for the night," Rick says as he stands up. "I should be doing that, too."

"Yeah, I guess they have the right idea," Quinn agrees as he rises out of his chair and starts to walk to the door. He says good-night to Rick. "We have early meetings tomorrow."

Rick nods. "See you then."

"I'll be inside," Quinn says to me as he opens the door and goes into the house.

I expect Rick to go home, but he sits down on the porch with me instead. He is no sooner seated than the porch light goes out.

"Again," I say. "Those bulbs must be defective."

"I don't think so," Rick says softly. "It's Quinn."

Rick doesn't know my brother very well if he thinks my brother turned the light off so the two of us could sit out here in the dark. But I don't say anything. I don't want to spoil the moment by going on about my overly protective sibling.

"I know you said you could handle things with the wedding," Rick says. The moon is not full tonight, but I can still see the outlines of his face. "But if you need help, I talked to some of the guys at the station and they're all willing to help do whatever. I figure you can direct us and together we'll pull this all off."

"There's not going to be a wedding," I say. "At least not one like the one we planned. Quinn and Marilee decided to do quick and simple."

The air feels a little chilly, but it's not too bad. I wrap my sweater around me, and I am fine. Of course, the weather doesn't matter. I wouldn't leave this porch right now even if there was a blizzard headed this way. Rick's eyes are dark pools of intense black, and they make me feel prickly inside.

"I heard that," Rick says and then pauses. "But I didn't think that would stop you."

"Well, they really should do more than they're planning," I say. "I'm afraid they'll regret not doing any of the traditional things if they don't."

Rick nods. "Then we should make some of them happen. What is the plan?"

"All I know is that the date's March thirty-first."

"That's next Saturday," he says. "We'd been talking about having our One Hundred and Five that evening," he says.

"Oh." That's not good. "I know Quinn wants the guys from the station to come to the wedding."

"I'll talk to the captain about moving the date of our

celebration," Rick says. "I could use more time to plan it right anyway."

"Thanks, but can you do that?"

"No one knows the exact day that lightbulb was made anyway, so its birthday can move around a bit," Rick continues.

"Just don't move it to April first," I say, hoping to lighten things up. "People have a hard enough time believing the bulb has been shining away that long anyway."

Rick grins. "I wouldn't believe it, either. I hope I don't need to work for a hundred years."

"A hundred and *five*," I add. "And people still don't want to give it a rest."

It's nice sitting here with Rick in the darkness. I know it's not the same as what Marilee and Quinn have going for them, but it does help me understand why they might forego an elaborate wedding so they can get married sooner.

"You've had your cancer checkup recently, haven't you?" Rick finally asks.

I nod. "Just a few months ago. I'm fine."

Rick moves a little closer and gives me a hug. "I'm glad."

I nod again, but there's just something romance-killing about always worrying about illness. I don't want to be the one Rick worries about. I want him to laugh and look at me the way he used to look at those women he brought around when he was nineteen—the ones he showed the Girl Scout cookies to. He wasn't feeling sorry for any of them.

I half expect it, so I'm not surprised when Rick

kisses the top of my head again before he stands up to go home.

I get up with him and watch as he walks down the brick path to the street. Then I turn to go inside the house. Once inside, I check on the porch light switch. What do you know? It is in the off position. I try the light just to be sure that it works, and it does. I can't believe it. The Old Mother Hen turned the light off. He must be more shook up inside than I suspected.

Quinn is sitting at the kitchen table, drinking a can of Coke. He's looking pretty drained, so I go over and put an arm around him. "I'm sorry."

He puts his hand up, and it covers the hand I have on his shoulder. "I can't lose her."

"I know." I hug him even closer. "Me, neither."

I move away a little and sit down in the chair next to him at the table. "But are you sure about not having a regular wedding? It's your one big day."

Quinn looks at me. "Marilee said she was okay with not doing the traditional walking down the aisle thing with the dress and the cake and all the other things."

"I know. And she is—sort of." I smile at my brother. "But only because she's a little scared. Part of her still thinks her dad left because of her cancer."

"I'd never leave."

"I know."

"She and I belong together."

I nod. "But you wouldn't object to a bigger wedding— if I can pull together some of the traditional things—as long as it all comes together on the thirty-first?"

"Of course I don't mind," he says. "I'd be grateful, and so would she."

I stand up. "I can't promise anything, so don't tell Marilee yet, but I'm going to do my best."

"Thank you," Quinn says, and I think he's close to tears sitting there. "I've always known I can count on you."

Actually, it's been the reverse, but I figure I'll let it stand. The poor guy is distressed and befuddled. I pat him on the shoulder and then kiss the top of his head. Giving him a kiss on the head like that feels full of sympathy and affection. I wonder if that's the way Rick feels when he kisses me that way.

I go to sleep that night looking at the outline my rose makes against my window in the dark. The flower is in full bloom now. I wonder if romantic love ever grows out of brotherly affection. I'll need to pray that it does.

The next morning I go to my Wednesday classes and then head over to the Pews. I want to find a way to consult with Marilee and make my final list for the wedding without her being suspicious. I think planning this wedding is going to be good therapy for me. It keeps my mind off Marilee's health.

I don't want to tell Marilee what I'm doing until I'm sure I can make it happen, though. I have gathered all of my coupons from the class, and I plan to start making calls this afternoon.

Marilee is in her office when I knock. She invites me in, and I can see she's at least trying to concentrate. She looks pale, but she has a spreadsheet in front of her.

"Work?" I ask.

She nods. "For some reason, we have a ton more crab meat in the freezer than we ordinarily do, and I'm trying to figure out what happened. I must have made a mistake on the order somewhere along the line."

Marilee does all of the ordering and bookkeeping for the diner. "I won't take much of your time," I tell her.

Marilee waves her hand. "Don't worry about it. We'll use up the crab. I'm just trying to keep myself busy."

I take out my notebook. "Then it's a good time to check with you about the invitations for the wedding. I figure we'll send a save-the-date invitation with directions to a Web site where your guests can get last-minute instructions and—"

"I'm so sorry we're doing this to you," Marilee interrupts me. "I just realized—this means you won't have a showcase wedding for your business."

"Oh, don't worry about that," I say. That's the least of my concerns now.

I reach into my book bag and pull out my school tablet. "Do you have any special wording you want for the invitation?"

"I'll write something out for you."

"And flowers," I add. "Even if you're only wearing a suit, you'll still want a small bouquet to hold."

"I've always wanted pink roses," Marilee says happily, and then she frowns. "Although maybe I should change that now, too. That suit of my mother's isn't a true beige. It has some kind of a gold cast to it. Maybe I should go with yellow flowers instead."

I can't help myself. "But you always wanted pink roses. I never once heard you talk about yellow anything."

"I know," Marilee says and then sighs.

"We'll do what we can," I assure Marilee.

I don't have the heart to ask Marilee about a cake.

Besides, I don't need any more details right now. I heard her wedding plans repeatedly many years ago. Nothing has changed.

I leave Marilee's office determined to do the impossible.

I drive over to a bakery on Foothill Boulevard and discover that the rumors in class were true; they do bake a glorious wedding cake with the kind of fondant-lace icing that Marilee has spoken of so fondly in the past. The cake they have on display looks almost Victorian with all of the delicate lacing. And, when they give me a taste of it, I almost swoon. It is vanilla cake with a raspberry filling that rivals the jam Marilee loves. It's the absolute perfect cake for her wedding.

God says we should come to Him with our hearts' desires, so I do. *Please, please, please, Lord. This is the one we want.*

Then I ask to see the manager. I had been given a half-off coupon in class for the bakery, but it was for a plain cake, not for the elaborate wedding cake that I now have my heart set on. I almost high-five the manager when he agrees to accept my coupon for the cake I want. I am delighted when the discount makes the bill low enough that I can pay for it myself. It'll be my wedding present to Quinn and Marilee. I even arrange for one of those cute bridal couples to stand on top of the cake, and the manager boxes up a sample of the cake so I can take it back to Marilee to get her official approval.

I feel like such a professional wedding planner when I leave the bakery that I decide to visit a bridal shop just off of Green Street. Marilee had given me her size and

the type of dress she'd wanted weeks ago. I feel foolish
to even try this shop. I know how exclusive it is. They
only have designer gowns and cater to brides who can
spend a few thousand dollars on their dress and not have
to cut back on any other part of their wedding. Obviously, I don't have a coupon of any kind for here. I
doubt they want customers who can't afford the full
price.

I love feeling the fabrics of these gowns. Satins, silks
and some lace that is feather soft. I am surprised that it
is hard to really look through the gowns, they are not
organized very well. The sizes are all mixed up, and the
gowns aren't even sorted by color. Everything's
jumbled like you'd expect it to be at a discount store. I
catch a glimpse of the back room, and it even looks like
a warehouse there. Gowns are hung all over these high
rods.

Still, there are more women in the place than the
person behind the counter can assist.

"You look like you could use some extra help," I say
when it's my turn to talk to the harried clerk.

The woman nods her head. "I just bought this shop,
and I'm waiting for my niece to get out of school in a
couple of months. She's supposed to help me organize
things. The sale wasn't supposed to go through so fast,
but when it did I just opened up. And I can't hire just
anyone to help, you know. A woman needs a certain
class to sell these dresses."

"Well, all I need is a price check," I say. I found one
dress that I think might be reasonable, but I don't know
because it's not marked.

"I keep meaning to close the shop for a day and get

tags on everything," the woman says. "But business has been good and—"

I take a deep breath. If I hadn't scored such a victory at the bakery, I probably wouldn't be so bold.

"I could help," I say. "I could organize while people are still shopping. That way you wouldn't need to miss any time at all."

"I don't know. I have a problem with cash flow at the moment. Like I said, the sale went through too fast. And then those gowns are so high up in the back. I can't even reach most of those hangers without a ladder."

"I can do ladders. I'll have everything organized in no time. And—" I can see she's weakening "—it won't cost you a penny. All I want in exchange is to use one of your dresses for a day—well, really for a day and a night."

The woman looks at me in surprise. "No one's ever asked—"

"It's a win-win deal," I say.

"Well, I do have a couple of dresses that have a little damage. I can't sell them as new stock. I suppose if you wanted to use one of those, it would be okay."

There are no other customers behind me in line, so the woman takes me into the back and quickly shows me the two dresses that are damaged. One of them has a torn sleeve, but it's the other one that grabs my interest. It's a Vera Wang cream-colored sheath that will fit Marilee perfectly. I'm afraid to ask if the lace is imported, but it's so lovely it must be. There are also pearls cascading down the back of the dress that form a point at the base of a small train. It's a princess dress if I've ever seen one.

"The hem is scorched a little," the woman says, and I can see it when I look. "According to the records, the woman actually had paid for the dress, so when she brought it back the other owner gave her a reduced price on a new dress. Of course, they couldn't return this one, and it's been hanging back here. You can smell the fire in the fabric still."

I dutifully sniff the dress and decide that some fresh roses will do away with the smoke smell.

I leave the store, wondering when I became so brave. I plan to spend next Tuesday working at the woman's store. She doesn't have a ladder, so I'll need to bring a small one. I might not be able to finish the whole reorganization in one day, but I will get it started.

I'm tired, but I drive back to the Pews so I can leave the cake sample on Marilee's desk. She's not there, but I leave a note asking her if this would do for the wedding cake. I don't tell her how big the cake will be or that I've arranged for the special icing.

I look at the Sisterhood journal before I go to bed. Marilee gave it back to me, but I can't seem to write anything in it. I sit on my bed in the light of my lamp and realize I don't know what to say. I am worried, and I think the reason I was so driven today is because I've spend a lot of my energy trying not to think of what's really worrying me. I wonder if I am so intent on giving Marilee a dream wedding because she might die.

In the darkness I fumble to find the Lizzie stone that sits on my nightstand, and I begin to rub it. I know I said I'd give up the stone, but I can't right now. Not when so much bad could be happening all around me.

My fears keep growing in my mind. What if Marilee is only the first one? What if we all relapse? Can we all do this again?

I don't want to write any of this in the journal, though. So I pick up my pen and write a little about the wedding.

I ordered a fondant-iced cake today for Marilee's wedding. And the most gorgeous Victorian wedding gown. I feel like I'm the fairy godmother getting ready for Cinderella. Marilee doesn't know she's going to the ball, but I do. I wonder what other surprises God has for us as we put together this wedding.

I finish writing in the journal, fold the page back, and put my pen on the nightstand. I don't dream at all during the night, and when I wake up, I lie in bed for a bit before going down for breakfast. I see that Rick left me a note, propped up against the sugar bowl on the kitchen table. He and Quinn carpool when their schedules match, and Quinn always runs inside to leave a note for Mom when he comes by to hook up with Rick.

"I'm here if you need me," the note from Rick reads.

Rick is a lot like Quinn. I can finally understand how Marilee feels. I don't want Rick to have to worry about me all of the time any more than she wants Quinn to worry about her.

For the first time since I've become a Christian, I leave the house that morning without praying.

Chapter Eleven

"A little simplification would be the first step
toward rational living…."

—Eleanor Roosevelt

*Our counselor, Rose, was the voice of experience
when we met. Back then she always said that she
hadn't lived to be forty without learning a thing or
two about life. We didn't know what to say when she
would say things like that. None of us in the Sisterhood knew if we'd live to see twenty-five. We couldn't
imagine turning forty.*

*Rose might have suspected what we were thinking,
but she didn't apologize. One of the things we liked
best about Rose was that she treated us like normal
people. She didn't try to avoid any mention of cancer
or the fears we faced. She took our illness in stride.
She didn't apologize for the fact that we might die
some day soon. Her acceptance of us, and our illness,
helped us deal with it.*

* * *

Rose is with us tonight. We are sitting in the Sisterhood room, feeling very grateful she's here. I suspect Becca called and asked her to come, but the older woman walked into the room like she'd just dropped by to say hello.

If Rose didn't know about Marilee before she stepped through the door, she found out two seconds later when Marilee went up to get a long, desperate hug from her. I knew by the way Rose patted Marilee on the back that the older woman had it all figured out.

Even with that, though, Marilee didn't want to talk about the possibility that her cancer might have come back.

"How bad is it?" Rose asks her quietly.

"Until I have the needle biopsy, I won't know," Marilee says flatly.

"Do you want to talk about it?" Rose asks.

Marilee just shakes her head. Truthfully, I'm not sure any of us want to talk about it. Not that we want to knit, either. Or talk. If there was more floor space around our table, I think we'd have all stood up and started to pace.

Finally, I remember that I have the invitations with me. Marilee gave me the text and the printer did them simply and quickly, so all we need to do now is fold the invitations and address the envelopes. Since Marilee has the list in her office of the addresses, we decide to sit and get the envelopes ready for mailing.

The invitations aren't embossed like we would have requested if we had more time, but the printer did use a nice paper and an elegant font.

"I can work with that Web site if you want," Becca

says as she reads the invitation and sees the note about the final location being posted online. "The kids at the shelter have fun putting those together."

Becca has been volunteering at that shelter for teenage kids for almost a year now and has learned some surprising things. She doesn't always rely on her goals and her lists like she used to; sometimes she plays it straight from the heart.

"That would be good," I say.

Talking about the invitations leads into a discussion about the wedding.

"So you're really not going to have the traditional thing at all?" Carly asks softly. "Not the veil or those cute pictures of you and Quinn feeding each other a piece of the cake?"

"We don't want to wait," Marilee says. "I don't know how much time I'll have with Quinn, so I want all I can get."

"Well, then it's sort of like an elopement," Carly says with a brightness to her voice that I know is forced. "That always be romantic in its own way. People used to do that all the time."

"No one invites sixty guests to their elopement," Marilee says, but she does give a smile, which is probably what Carly wanted. "Besides, we'll do the big, splashy ceremony on our fifth anniversary. That'll work out fine."

Everyone is silent at that announcement. I wonder if the other sisters are wondering the same thing I am. What if Marilee's cancer is back? Will she be here for her fifth anniversary?

I feel a sudden pang. Quinn would feel really bad if

Marilee never got her celebration; we all would. I need to make this wedding happen in the right way.

"Five years? That'll give you something to look forward to," Rose says kindly.

"Yes," I say, even if it is too quickly.

Becca and Carly murmur agreement.

Just then Uncle Lou brings us in a big pot of tea, and by unspoken agreement we start to talk about the flavor of the various biscotti he sets down on the table along with the cups. We can always count on Uncle Lou to know when we need something extra for our meetings.

When we've finished our tea, Marilee asks if we mind spending some time praying. We all bow our heads and plead with God, sometimes silently and sometimes aloud.

I am ashamed that I still have the Lizzie stone in my pocket. I've been carrying it around telling myself I am only looking for a place to leave the rock. But the fact that I can't find a place good enough for it makes me wonder if that is only an excuse to keep it close to me. I tell myself that soon, after I get the wedding details nailed down and find out about Marilee's health, I will read one of those books on prayer that the pastor gave me. Maybe if I understand how to make prayer work better, I won't miss having the Lizzie stone in my life.

I notice Marilee doesn't have a baseball cap on today, so I know she is winning her battle. She's probably praying all of the time now, too. I feel like I'm back in kindergarten and not learning as fast as the other kids. Can one fail at being a Christian?

Carly offers to walk with me to my car after the Sisterhood meeting. She's parked in a different lot, and I plan to drive her to her car once we reach mine. I find the walk down the dark street relaxing.

"I can't believe Marilee and Quinn aren't going to do some things for their wedding," Carly says. "Not after all of those plans Marilee had for all of these years. I think her wedding dreams kept her alive back when she had cancer. I'll never forget her talking about the frosting on that cake one night. I could almost taste it."

We are walking past the candle shop, and I stop to breathe in the jumbled fragrance of spices and flowers. One thing cancer gave me an appreciation for was the many smells and tastes in life.

"I'm still hoping to put together something for them," I finally say. "In fact, I've lined up a fabulous bridal gown and a wedding cake that's out of this world. I gave Marilee a sample of the cake last week, and she agreed it was perfect, but she doesn't know how big the cake that I ordered is. Most of it's still a secret because, until we find a place to have this wedding, it can't happen like I picture it. In fact, it might not happen at all."

"Oh, I'm so glad you're going forward with it," Carly says. "I think it's important. I mean, I know that they want to marry soon, and I can understand that, but—"

"Yeah, I know."

"If there's anything I can do to help, just let me know," Carly says.

"Well, if you have any ideas about where we can have a wedding with sixty guests, let me know."

"Uncle Lou would close the Pews for the night if we asked him," Carly says.

"I thought of that. But there's no place inside the

diner to make an aisle for a bride to walk down. And let's face it—the place looks so much like what it is that it's hard to imagine it as a wedding chapel."

We all love the Pews, but it's not one of those trendy restaurants that could double as a supper club. It would be like Cinderella having the ball in the kitchen she had just scrubbed. Even if she was wearing her new dress and shoes, it wouldn't be the same.

Carly grins. "I forgot about Marilee and her wedding aisle fantasy. She used to go on and on about the rose petals in the aisle and the others falling down from the sky while she walked down the aisle and the ribbons from her rose corsage trailed along as she went."

I nod. "She's always gone overboard with roses. She wanted them on the cake, on the tables, on the groom—everywhere."

"Well, we'll find someplace that works with roses. Is anybody else helping with this?"

I'm quiet for a second before I tell her. "Rick offered to help, and he said some of the other firefighters would, as well."

"I hope you told him yes," Carly says as we walk into the main floor of the parking structure.

I shake my head. "I don't want him to always feel like he has to rescue me. Like I'm just a kid who gets into trouble and can't get out on my own. It's depressing."

We take the elevator up to the roof of the parking structure and get into my car.

"I don't think that's how he sees you," Carly says as we both fasten our seat belts. "He wouldn't ask you out to a place like the Ritz-Carlton if he just felt sorry for you."

"Really?" I turn to her. The inside of my car is dark, but I can still see her face because of the security lights.

"Absolutely not."

I trust Carly to know men, but something still rankles. "He's never kissed me, you know. Not on the lips. He's kissed my forehead and the top of my head, but never the lips."

"Not even after we did that makeover? And you went out to dinner?"

I shake my head.

"Well, I suppose there's some reason for that," Carly says slowly. "Guys are all different."

She doesn't sound nearly as confident of her opinion, though, as she did earlier.

It takes only a couple of minutes to drop Carly off at her car and then I am headed back home. I decide I will probably never know what Rick is up to. Maybe it has nothing at all to do with me. Maybe he took me to the Ritz-Carlton as a practice run for some other dinner he planned to have there. Or he might just be rattling Quinn's cage in some way. He must know that my brother doesn't like anyone to date me. Maybe Rick is teaching Quinn a lesson.

I sigh. Rick might even be doing it for kind reasons. He has obviously been looking out for me for years. Maybe he figures if Quinn gets used to seeing him with me, my brother will let me date anyone I want. Which would be a good and kind deed on Rick's part. The only problem is that it's becoming increasingly clear to me that the only one I want to date is Rick.

That night I look through my book bag and pull out one of the books on prayer that the pastor gave me. I open it but stop reading at the first page. Instead, I close my eyes and start to pray.

Now that I can't really ask my Lizzie stone for help, I throw myself on the mercies of God. There are so many things that need to be straightened out in my life, and even though I know how they should look once they're fixed, I don't have a clue about how to make them change. There's Marilee, of course, at the top of the list. And my relationship with Rick. And my sympathy for Quinn. Oh, and the wedding. I go to sleep in the confidence that God knows and will make everything happen just the way I need. I sleep peacefully.

The next morning I am up and ready in plenty of time to pick Marilee up for her mammogram. I meet her at the Pews again and sit with a cup of tea while she finishes her breakfast.

"I better get this figured out soon," she says to me as we sit at the counter. "The way Uncle Lou is feeding me, I'll have a weight problem if this all goes on much longer."

I smile. We both know that it's hard on the people who love us when we're sick. Everyone wants to help a sick person, and all too often there's not much they can do. So they end up feeding them or, in the case of someone like Quinn, watching their every move in case they need any little speck of help tying their shoelaces or something.

We go to the same doctor's office that we visited on Tuesday. The same receptionist is on duty, and I go over to say hello only to realize she has problems of her own.

"Allergies," she says with a sniffle. "I've been sneezing all day."

The woman's eyes and nose are red.

"I hope you feel better," I say as I walk back to the chairs. The woman looks like she has more than allergies to me, but I'm not a doctor. I spend the rest of the time flipping through a *Glamour* magazine that's a few years old. I'm in the middle of taking their "Is He the One?" quiz when my cell phone rings.

It's Quinn, and he wants to know what's happening.

"You just called ten minutes ago," I say as I mark Yes on the question about similar tastes in movies. Neither Rick nor I go to many movies, so we have that in common.

"Well, has anything happened?"

"Nothing's going to happen today." I repeat what I told him earlier. "The doctor won't read the film until later."

I have barely hung up with Quinn when Carly calls to let me know that she has tried to contact all the city parks that are close enough to Pasadena to be possibilities for a wedding. I have been hopeful because I know some of them have sheltered areas that would hold sixty people.

"Good news?" I ask.

"Not a bit," Carly says. "I called every one of them, and half of them say no weddings right on their messages. The other half just wait and say it in person."

"Well, surely we're not the only people around who want to find a cheap place for a small wedding. What do people like us do?"

"They plan ahead and go to churches."

Carly and I had both tried all of the churches we thought might be possibilities. The one that we attend out in Sierra Madre doesn't have any Saturdays open for weddings until the middle of May. The few churches that do have openings for March thirty-first are more expensive than Descanso Gardens.

"Oh, I've got to go," I say to Carly. I see Marilee coming out of the back offices again.

The mammogram was routine, and, like I expected, she doesn't have any new information. Now that I am trying to remember to go to God with my worries, I ask Marilee if we can pray while we sit out in my car at the doctor's office.

I boldly pray for Marilee to be healed, for her to grow old with my brother, for them to be happy together for many years. Marilee holds my hand as I talk to God.

Once we do that, I drive back to Pasadena and drop Marilee off at the Pews so she can finish the bookkeeping for the week. Then I head over to the college to put up a notice on the bulletin board asking for a violin student to play for a small wedding. I even stop and pray before I put the notice up, asking God to bring us a really good violin player.

All day I pray, pray, pray. I haven't been this tired in a long time, though. My mother is away for the weekend visiting my aunt in San Diego, so I decide to go home and fall into bed early.

I wake up in the morning with a raw throat and a sinking feeling. I never even thought to pray that I wouldn't get sick. My face feels feverish and my eyes hurt. I won't be able to go anywhere and look at anything related to the wedding. This couldn't have happened at a worse time. I have the bridal gown to take care of, a location to find, and the flowers—oh dear, I haven't even called any florists.

I would never say it in public, but I am a little disappointed in God. He should have known I needed to stay well for the next two weeks without me telling Him. It's hard enough to pray for the good things that need to happen, it's almost impossible to pray for all of the bad things that might happen at the same time. Do I need to pray that the sun rises in the morning and sets at night? I should be able to count on God for some things.

Well, I finally decide, *I can't stay in bed all morning worrying about what might happen.* So I pull my cell phone out of my purse and call Carly.

"We've got problems," I say flat out. Well, I try to say it flat out. My voice doesn't cooperate very well, though, and my words are a little muffled. "Sick."

"I'm on my way over," she says.

"No, no," I say. "Need you well."

If Carly and I are both sick, who will find a place to have this wedding? And take care of Marilee when she has her needle biopsy? And—

I realize whom I really need to call.

"Quinn," I say when he answers from the safety of his condo. "Don't come over. Sick. Stay well. Marilee needs—"

My words aren't too clear, but I think he understands. At least, he ends the conversation by agreeing that he needs to stay healthy and so won't come by today.

I fall back onto my pillows once I have warned everyone away. I'll rest a bit and then get up and take my temperature.

I must have fallen asleep, because I wake up to a pounding on the front door. I figure whoever it is will go away, but it continues, so I go to my window to look down at the porch to see who is creating the racket.

It's Rick, holding a white container and looking up at my window.

He puts his hands around his mouth and yells. "Coming in."

Rick knows that Mom keeps a spare house key in the bottom of the bird house on the corner of the porch. I see him walk over to it now that he has my attention.

This is not good, I tell myself.

I wrap a blanket around myself and pull my slippers on so I can go downstairs and tell him to flee this germ-infested house. I feel like I need a leper's bell.

"Sick," I try to say as I reach the bottom of the stairs. Rick is sitting at the kitchen table in that old gray jogging suit for which I've grown to have a particular fondness even though he really should cut it up and use it for waxing his car or scrubbing his kitchen floor.

"I know you're sick. That's why I'm here," Rick says cheerfully. He's got that white container in front of him. "I never catch colds, and when Quinn called, we thought you might need some soup—"

"We?" Ah, it smells like Japanese miso soup. I love that stuff.

All of a sudden my temperature is starting to rise and I know it's not from the cold. I am standing here with my hair matted around my head and looking like a refugee wrapped in this old beige blanket. But Rick must have gone to that place on Foothill Boulevard and brought me my favorite soup. This has to mean something, I tell myself. Something serious. Knights of old might have slain dragons for their ladies, but my personal hero just walked into a germ-infested house to bring me miso soup.

I think he loves me. Maybe. Maybe. *Oh, please, God, make it so.*

"Thank you," I say, wondering if the ladies in olden days were more eloquent when their knights presented them with a freshly defeated dragon. "Very much."

I don't have a smear of makeup on my face, and my eyelashes are probably lost in the pallor of my skin, but I beam at Rick anyway. Maybe he's had the real kind of love for me all along and I just haven't seen it.

My heart beats faster. God must have heard my pleas. My prayers must be answered. Hallelujah! Just like in the Bible.

"Thank you," I say once again.

"It's the least I can do," Rick says calmly as he opens the white container. "Besides, you would do the same for me. That's what friends do. They help each other."

Okay, I can go with that. "Friends."

Now Rick looks at me, and his face gets all solemn. "I know we haven't always seen eye to eye, but since Quinn is getting married, I'm hoping we can become better friends."

Oh. "Better friends?" I try to say.

Rick nods.

"I think Quinn would like that," Rick says as he stands up. "Here, let me get you a bowl for that soup."

So this is why Rick is being so nice to me. He wants me to morph into a version of Quinn once my brother is married and not able to spend as much friend time with him as before. I suppose I'm just convenient because I live next door, too.

I think my throat has swollen up. I can barely swallow any of the soup, not even when Rick pours it into a bowl for me and gives me one of the big spoons from my mother's silverware drawer.

What just happened here? I prayed for Rick to love me, and God did nothing. Isn't He supposed to answer my prayers? Maybe I did something wrong in the way I said things. I should have read more than the first page of that book on prayer. There must be some technique I didn't use. Like saying "Please" or "Pretty please." I guess I shouldn't expect to just take off praying and have things turn out very well.

I manage to eat half of the soup before telling Rick a final thank-you and starting back up the stairs. I have a long day ahead of me, and I need to figure out how to ask God for things before this whole wedding—not to mention my life—falls apart any more than it already has.

Friends? How can Rick think I want to just be friends? Has he forgotten that I proposed to him when I was only seven years old? Did that sound like I wanted to be friends? Even I knew better than that, and I was only seven.

Chapter Twelve

"People don't have fortunes left them in that style
nowadays; men have to work and women to marry
for money. It's a dreadfully unjust world."
—Louisa May Alcott

*Rose brought us this quote one night. I think she was
trying to cheer us up. Or maybe she just wanted to
put all of our wedding talk in perspective. Maybe
because reality was so grim for us, we tended to have
lush fantasies filled with beautiful clothes and perfect
heroes. Life, she said, was a mixture of the beautiful
and the plain, of things that were whole and those
that were broken. In the final result, she said, there is
very little fairness about it all. Not, she added with the
confidence of one who knew, that life isn't a grand
adventure anyway.*

I'm not prepared for defeat. Rick has been in my life
since before I learned to walk, and even though I would

never have admitted it, I have always felt that someday he would be my one true love. He was the groom in all of my wedding fantasies. He was meant to be with me.

I'm so sure of this, and yet, as I hold open that book on prayer, I wonder why God doesn't just make things happen that way if it's supposed to be. Does He want me to get down on my knees and beg? Write Him a poem and recite it? Fight a Philistine?

I'm willing to work with Him here, but I need some direction. It's altogether discouraging, and I'm tired. The wild parrots don't come to roost this evening even though I try to stay awake to listen for them.

When I wake up the next morning, I take a minute to erase the jumble of my night dreams. I put my hand on my forehead to get some sense of whether or not I still have a fever. I have too many things to do to spend another day in bed. I might not have a true love waiting for me, but Marilee does. Given my own disappointment in love, I am more determined than ever that Marilee will have the fantasy wedding she used to dream about. One of us needs to do this for all of us. We cannot just let our dreams die, not when we held on so tightly to them when we were sick.

I look at my clock. Carly and Becca will both be in church about now. I'll have to wait to call them. Carly told me that the pastor is going to have a special prayer for Marilee today, so I'm glad everyone can be there. Since I can't get this prayer business right, I'm happy to let the professionals do it.

In the meantime, I'm going to do what I said I'd do— plan a wedding. It's plain that I'm going to need help, but Becca and Carly won't let me down. Somehow, between the three of us, we'll find a way to make this wedding happen.

It's four hours later before I realize we're going to have problems. Neither one of the other sisters can take the time on Tuesday to go and work for the woman with the bridal gowns. Carly has to cover for Uncle Lou while he has a dental appointment, and Becca has a test. The woman might be open to changing the date for when the gowns are organized, but I don't really want to call her and give her a chance to back out altogether. By now she may have decided I'm some crazy lady.

"Is there anyone else?" Carly asks when we talk. "You mentioned Rick said the other firefighters were willing to help. Maybe one of them has a wife or girlfriend that would go in and help the woman."

"I don't want to ask Rick," I croak out. Maybe when I'm feeling better, I will tell Carly about how it is between him and me, but I don't have the voice to do it now.

"We're going to need help," Carly says. "And he brought you that soup. I know he cares."

"Maybe Quinn can help," I say. My brother knows the same firemen that Rick does. If the men want to help with the wedding, I don't see what difference it makes if Quinn or Rick asks them.

Thankfully, Carly accepts that as a solution, so I call Quinn and leave him a message to call me. Not wanting to spend any more time in bed, I wrap myself in a blanket and pick up the book on prayer to take down to the living room to read. At the last minute, I pick up the Sisterhood journal and bring it, too.

Two hours later I'm sitting there with tears streaming down my face. I didn't know most of these things about prayer. I have been going about it all wrong.

I thought my problem was just that I needed to stop using the Lizzie stone and start praying instead, but that's not at the heart of it at all. The problem is that I have been using prayer like it *was* my Lizzie stone. I might have been praying, but I wasn't listening. All I was really doing was telling God what He should do. Whether it was prayer or the Lizzie stone, I still wanted to be in control, especially on the big things.

What does that reduce God to? Some kind of cosmic wish-giver? I could have as easily been bowing down to Alfred, our waiter at the restaurant, ordering him to solve my problems like I had options on the menu of life.

This book right here says that a prayerful heart is one that waits for God to do His will. It's not about telling God what to do; it's about trusting Him and accepting what He wants.

I sit here with my feverish head and realize God may have a different plan for my life than the one I had always imagined. And I'm not talking about the little details. I take a deep breath and brace myself. Maybe Rick is not supposed to be anything more to me than a friend. Maybe I am not the woman for him and he's not the man for me.

I feel the breath leave me slowly. Being a Christian is harder than I ever imagined. I didn't realize how it'd feel to give up my way with things.

I put the book down on the sofa and pick up the Sisterhood journal. I need to record this insight. So I write—

God has opinions. He's not a puppet. I learned today that He's not up there relying on me to give

Him instructions on how He needs to fix things down here. I'm not sure how I feel about this, but I will write about it later.

I truly don't know how I feel. I need to start reading the Bible so I can learn about God the right way instead of relying on the vague notions I have in my head.

When Quinn knocks at the door a couple of hours later with a bag of fresh oranges, I am doing better. My fever is gone and I can talk more clearly.

My brother has the good sense not to come inside, but he does talk to me through the screen door.

I don't tell him why I called earlier, though. I've decided that, if I'm going to be Rick's friend, I need to ask him for the help instead of my brother. Rick is right; friends do things for each other.

"You've got everything else you need?" Quinn asks as he opens the door a little so he can put the oranges inside. "Rick said he'd bring soup."

"He did and I'm fine," I say.

"See that you eat lots of those," Quinn says as he nods at the oranges. "You need to get better if you're going to go with Marilee on Wednesday."

I nod and am quiet for a minute before I say, "Rick's been a good friend to you, hasn't he?"

"He sure has." Quinn pauses for a bit and then adds, "You eat those oranges now."

"I'll do that," I promise.

Quinn leaves after a few minutes, and I decide to go back to bed. Before I do, though, I dutifully sit down and peel an orange. Once I eat it, I peel another. No one will be able to say I didn't do what I could to get well. Once I get into bed, I pick up my Bible and start to pray. I know God is okay with asking, and so I ask Him for Marilee's health. I go to sleep thinking about her.

On Monday, I set up command central. I'm feeling better and the wedding is less than a week away. I put on a pair of sweats and wash my face. Then I call Marilee on her cell phone.

"How are you feeling?" I try to make my voice sound casual. It's a little after nine, so I know Marilee will be at work.

"Like I just got off Space Mountain at Disneyland," she says with a tilt to her voice. "Quinn came by the house this morning and serenaded me. My mother didn't know what was going on. Isn't that romantic?"

"Wonderful," I say. I know for a fact that my brother sings off-key.

Marilee sighs. "He's so good to me."

Yeah, well—

"Say, I didn't get a chance to ask earlier, but do you two have someone to perform your wedding?" I hear some talking in the background, so I figure she's eating her breakfast at the Pews.

"Oh dear, no," Marilee says. She doesn't sound dreamy-eyed any longer. "Quinn and I should have done that, shouldn't we? We meant to ask Pastor Engstrom, but—"

Even with all of the noise, I can hear her quick breaths over the phone, and I know she's starting to panic.

"That's okay, I'll ask him," I rush in to promise. "You've got other things to think about."

I'm sorry now I even brought it up.

"You're still coming Wednesday, aren't you?" Marilee says. She's pitching her voice low so she won't be overheard. "When I go for the needle biopsy?"

I stop myself before I answer yes. I did a lot of thinking last night. We have overcome so much in the Sisterhood, and at times it feels like we did it all by ourselves through sheer determination. This brought us so close together we feel like we can do anything. I'm not sure that those bonds shouldn't be a little looser now, though.

If I'm going to step down so God can be in control of my life, maybe I need to let Him change things in other places, too. Maybe we all do.

"I think Quinn should go with you Wednesday," I say softly.

Marilee is silent, and then she says, "But it's always been the Sisterhood facing these doctors together. We're the team. We're the ones who know."

"You can always count on us. It's just that maybe Quinn needs to be front and center now and we sisters need to be in the wings. We'll always be there, but—well, you know, sort of behind Quinn, supporting you both."

"Did he say something to you?" Marilee asks. "I probably should have asked him to come, but—"

"No, he didn't say anything. He just wants everything to be okay for you. It was my idea. I mean, now that you're getting married—"

"I love him so much," Marilee says. Her voice overflows with it. "I thought about asking him to come, but in the Sisterhood we've always done it this way. I didn't want you to think I don't need you."

"I know. But you and Quinn—that's the way it should be."

I think about Marilee's words after we hang up. Her voice was so full of love for my brother that it literally shook. Someday I would like to have that kind of love for the man God has chosen for me. I suppose that, if it ever happens, I'll have questions about how to make him a part of my life as well.

In the meantime, I am going to learn how to be a friend to Rick Kiefer. One thing I do know is that friends don't worry about impressing each other. I don't need to pretend with him that I have things more together than they are. He may as well see my disorganized plans for this fantasy wedding that's totally unrealistic and probably hopeless.

I call him on his cell phone, and he answers on the first ring. "Lizzie. How are you?"

"Better," I say. I take a deep breath and go for it. "Can you come next door? I have a favor to ask."

"Sure," he says, sounding more pleased than I thought he would.

"We can talk through the screen door," I say. "I don't want you to get sick."

"I've already been exposed. Besides, I never get colds. I'll be right over."

I only have time to run a brush through my hair and change my T-shirt before I hear him knocking at the door.

I open the door and see him standing there with an open carton of apricot juice.

"I wasn't sure if you were getting enough fluids, so I brought this," he says as he holds out the carton. "There are a few glasses left."

"Thanks." I take the carton and open the door wide.

It's no surprise that we end up heading toward the kitchen table. The living room furniture doesn't get much use in my mother's house, not when the kitchen table is available.

"I'm hoping your offer is still open," I say when we've both sat down. I put the carton of juice on the table. "I need help with the wedding ceremony. I'm in a bit of a bind."

"I'm ready to go. Just let me know what you want me and the guys to do."

I hesitate. "I need some things moved."

That doesn't sound too bad, so I continue. "And you'll need ladders to reach some of the items."

"No problem. We'll do it. What is it? Tables? Boxes? Did you find a place to have the wedding? We can set up chairs if you need."

I shut my eyes. "I haven't found the location yet. What I need moved is wedding gowns."

He's silent for so long that I open my eyes. He's just sitting there looking puzzled.

"Did you say wedding gowns?" he asks.

I'm not sure I can ever really be just friends with this man. His hair is a little ruffled, and he looks like he's been outside riding his bike or something. Whatever the cause, I have an urge to smooth his hair down and I'm pretty sure none of his other friends would be feeling that about now.

I almost sigh, but I swallow instead. "Yeah, the lacy, frothy, white kind. Most of them are in plastic covers, of course, but—"

I watch as the confusion clears from Rick's face and

a smile teases the corners of his mouth. "Quinn put you up to this, didn't he? You're joking, right?"

Oh boy. "No, I'm afraid not. I'm trading services with this woman at a bridal shop. We organize her old inventory, and Marilee gets to borrow a beautiful wedding dress. I know it might not seem like much, but we can't let her wear her mother's old suit. It might be different if she had some sentimental attachment to the suit, but she doesn't, and it's beige and doesn't go with pink roses and—"

I trail off. I can't even look at Rick. Here is where he should realize he can't be friends with a girl.

Rick is silent for so long that I finally have to look at him in case he's gone into cardiac arrest or something. When I see his face, I wonder if something has gone wrong. He's not scowling at all. In fact, he has a little bit of the expression Marilee has on her face when she talks about her wedding dreams.

"What's wrong?" I ask.

"Nothing. I'm just thinking how every man secretly dreams of seeing his wife walking toward him in one of those dresses."

"You're kidding, right?"

He shakes his head. "Quinn will always remember seeing Marilee in a dress like that."

"Then maybe if you tell the guys they're doing it for Quinn, they'll be fine with moving those dresses."

Rick chuckles. "I'm not sure I should tell them anything until I get them there. Even if I did tell them, they wouldn't believe me. Especially Jake."

"Well, I won't feel sorry for him. He owes me for telling everyone what I said in the diner. That was a private moment, and he was eavesdropping."

"Yeah, well, he's been threatening to invite you out to dinner to make up for the fact," Rick says. "If Quinn wasn't so distracted, he would put an end to that idea."

"I don't know what Quinn's so excited about," I say. "It's only dinner. And I don't even have to go."

"Of course you're not going," Rick says.

I start to count to ten, but only make it to four. "I hope you're not going to bug me like Quinn always does. The last thing I need is another Old Mother Hen around."

Rick is silent for a minute. Maybe I need to read a book on how to talk to my friends, too.

"I guess you're entitled to go to dinner with whomever you want," Rick finally says. "I would simply suggest you make it lunch at the Pews."

"That's not very much like a date."

"It's close enough," he says.

I think I'm starting to get a headache.

"We can talk later," I finally say. "I've got to make some more calls."

After Rick leaves, I rub my temples. I really don't want to have Rick standing in for Quinn. My brother is probably behind the whole thing. No doubt he asked Rick to look out for me. Which means I'll have to talk to them both. Not that I have time to do anything right now.

I need to call up the woman with the bridal shop, explain that I'm sick, and tell her that several of my associates will be there to help her reorganize her inventory on Tuesday. When I do that, she only asks if they have ladders, and I assure her they do. I leave her my phone number in case she has any questions, and she tells me she's got the dress I want boxed up for me.

Pastor Engstrom is my next call.

"This Saturday?" he asks. "That's perfect. I just had a cancellation. Where is it?"

"I'll have to get back to you with the location."

He asks me how I'm doing, and I tell him some of my discoveries about prayer. He doesn't seem surprised that I've had to learn a few things. He says we'll talk about it in our next meeting.

I spend the rest of the day at the kitchen table making lists and praying. I figure the lists are possibilities and not demands that I am making of God;, hopefully, that will work for Him. I'm trying to be flexible.

I'm getting ready for bed that night when the phone rings. It's Rick.

"I just wanted to check and make sure you're okay," he says all in a rush. "Call me if you need anything and I'll bring it right over."

"Thanks," I say. "I already drank more of the apricot juice."

"Glad to hear that," he says in a voice that sounds about as strained as it gets.

"Look, about earlier," I say. "I'm sorry. Friends are entitled to worry about each other. If you think I'm going out with someone who will be unpleasant, you should be able to tell me."

"Really? Thanks." He sounds surprised. "Although I'm not sure I'd call Jake unpleasant. He might be too pleasant when it comes down to it. I just don't think he's steady."

"Well," I swallow. "You should be able to say whatever you think—just as long as that's all it is—your opinion."

I guess that works for him, because we say a cordial goodbye.

When we hang up, I try to discipline my mind. Friends don't sigh to themselves at the end of a conversation; they don't even usually replay the words in their mind a half dozen times wondering if they missed some special intonation from the other. They don't sit here, twisted in a knot, wondering why their friend objected to them going out with a certain other person in the first place.

Chapter Thirteen

> "'Stay' is a charming word in a friend's vocabulary."
> —Louisa May Alcott

Carly's mother sent this quote to us one evening. After a few months, all of our family members knew we took a few minutes at the start of our Sisterhood meetings to discuss a quote, and they were all looking for good ones.

Especially in those first meetings, we found that the words of strangers helped us talk to each other about how we were feeling in our lives. One of the things that brought us together, even early on, was the promise of friendship. For weeks after we read this quote together, we would ask each other to stay and smile when we said it. We did a lot of silly things back then to take our minds off the doctors and the chemo and the fear, but "Please stay" was one of our favorites.

It's Wednesday afternoon and I'm sitting in the Sisterhood room at the Pews waiting for Quinn and Marilee to get back from her doctor's appointment. Carly is working the counter out front and Becca is taking some test in one of her law classes. I'm over my cold and glad to be back with people.

I stayed home for four, almost five, days, and the world went on just fine without me. I've come to believe that maybe God planned it that way. Rick has taken over a lot of the wedding details, and he seems to be doing just as good as I could have with everything. Which would be a little depressing if I hadn't already made my peace with God about it.

I was supposed to be proving I am a grown-up by taking charge of this wedding fantasy, but as it turns out I learned more about being a grown-up by letting God and Rick handle things than I would have by insisting on doing everything myself.

Of course, the details are not all in place yet. We don't even have a location for the ceremony.

I look at my watch. Rick is supposed to be meeting me here in a few minutes to give me *The Dress*. Marilee still doesn't know anything about it. I think we'll tell her at the Sisterhood meeting tomorrow night.

Here Rick is now.

I can see him through the windows of the French doors as he fumbles to open the doors while holding on to a big box. That looks promising. I stand up and walk over to let him in.

"Have you heard anything?" Rick says the minute he gets inside. "I've been praying for Quinn and Marilee all morning."

"Me, too. But I haven't heard. In fact, we probably

won't hear for sure until Friday. The lab needs to do their thing and—"

Rick sets the box on the table and looks at me closely. "So how are you doing?"

"I'm good. I ate all those oranges and the apricot juice you left. Then I took some zinc. The combination knocked the cold out of me."

I look over at the box. "That's from the bridal shop?"

"Yeah. I can't believe we were such a hit at that place," Rick says. "Some of the guys even started to make suggestions to the women about what kind of a dress they should be wearing for their big day."

"Really?" Now, that could be good or bad. I decide I'd better open the box to be sure it contains what it's supposed to.

"They sure don't skimp on their packaging," I say as I pull a thin gold ribbon off the slick white box. I barely lift the lid when I see white tissue paper peeking out. When I take the lid higher, I see a cream-colored envelope sitting in the middle of the inside of the box.

I pick up the note and read it.

"I never sold so many gowns in three hours," the woman had written. "You're welcome to keep the dress. Thank you, and I hope you come in for your own wedding dress some day soon. I'll give you a great deal. The guys were fantastic. Allison Bennett, owner of Fine Bridal Wear."

"Wow," I say as I look up from the note. "I guess you and the guys really did do good."

"I tried to tell you," Rick says with a big smile.

I lift the dress up a little. Small ivory pearls nestle against the soft satin sheen of the gown's back. A lacy

veil is tucked under the dress that matches the ivory
color perfectly. A small edging of delicate lace outlines
the sleeves. The gown is stunning.

"You have no idea what this will mean to Marilee."

"Oh," Rick says with a soft smile, "I think I do. My
mom used to talk about how much she missed because
she didn't have a wedding dress."

Just then Carly comes into the room and gives a little
squeal. "Is this it?"

I lift the dress up even more so Carly can see it.

"Oh, it's absolutely beautiful," she says as she runs
her hand over the pearl beading on the back. "This is
just the kind of dress Marilee always talked about.
Romantic and classic—like Audrey Hepburn in those
old movies."

Carly looks at Rick. "Marilee's going to love it. I
can't believe you and Lizabett got the guys to do what
you did. Which reminds me—Uncle Lou told me to tell
you all of the guys are invited to drink coffee free here
for the month."

"Hey, thanks. He might be sorry he ever said that,
though. We can drink a lot of coffee."

"Yeah, well, Uncle Lou will do anything for
Marilee," Carly says.

We're all quiet for a minute. We'd all do anything
for her, too.

"I keep thinking they'll call," Carly finally says. "I
can't stand this waiting."

"Maybe we could pray for a bit," I say. I never
thought I would be the one suggesting we turn to God,
but I am trying to learn to trust Him, and prayer is a big
part of that.

We sit at the table, holding hands for comfort, and pray for Marilee's health and happiness. I try to picture God holding Marilee in His hands.

After we pray, I go find Uncle Lou. There was a plastic bag at the bottom of the box. I slip that over the dress and ask him to hide it in the storage area. He's delighted to do it.

Of course, I have to take Becca to the storage room when she comes in a little later. Talking about the dress gives everyone something to think about instead of Marilee's biopsy.

Uncle Lou brings us a pot of tea in the Sisterhood room, but he doesn't sit with us. It's the middle of the afternoon and he has a few customers out front. Besides, I know he likes to be busy.

It's fifteen or so minutes before we hear Marilee and Quinn talking as they come in the main door of the diner. Becca is closest to the French doors and she opens them so Marilee and Quinn can come inside the Sisterhood room with the rest of us.

They both look exhausted.

"We don't know anything yet," Marilee says before we even ask. "The doctor said we shouldn't worry, though. Usually, these kinds of lumps aren't cancerous—mostly they're fatty tissue or cysts."

Marilee has faint circles around her eyes, and her skin looks pale. I can't tell if she believes what the doctor told her or not.

Carly and I both stand up and walk toward Marilee. Becca is already close to her. We start to make one of our circle hugs, but Marilee stops before the four of us come together. She opens her arms to let Quinn into the hug, which leaves Rick standing there looking like an extra part to something, so I open my arms and welcome him into the group hug as well. It takes a minute, but we are finally together. I like the way it feels. We pull each other closer until we are in a huddle, with our heads bowed until they are almost touching in the middle of the circle.

Quinn is the one who starts to pray.

"Lord, give us strength," he says. "Remind us of Your love for each of us, and especially for Marilee."

Quinn pauses, and Carly takes up the prayer, "We ask Your good and perfect will in this as in all things."

I don't know the words to pray aloud, but I feel a surge in my heart. The book on prayer I read talked about the power of people praying together, but I never really experienced it until now. I wonder why I ever thought my Lizzie stone could do anything. That rock is dead, and this feels so alive.

"We remind You that You said when two or more are gathered in Your name, You would be there," Becca adds, and I smile. It's so like her to remind God of His promises. She's a lawyer in all things.

There's something comforting about seeing the way Becca is herself with God. It makes me feel better about the fact that I'm not the perfect Christian, either. Maybe God understands and accepts me more than I think He does.

Marilee's face is shining with tears by the time we say our final amens and break apart our hug.

"I can't thank you enough," Marilee says, so we each hug her again.

After we step back from her, Marilee excuses herself to go find Uncle Lou and let him know what the doctor said.

When the French doors close, I turn to Quinn. "She's telling us everything, isn't she? The doctor didn't add anything or—"

Quinn shakes his head. "I was with her when she talked to the doctor, and he said the odds are that it isn't cancerous. He's putting a rush on the lab work, though, because he knows we won't sleep until we know."

I have seen Quinn worried before, and he seems stronger this time.

"You really believe she'll be okay, don't you?" I ask him quietly.

He nods. "I know God is in control."

I hope that someday I will have a faith that is as strong as Quinn's. I look over at Rick, and I see him watching Quinn as well. We both have a lot to learn about this new life we've begun.

We all sit around the Sisterhood room for a few minutes until Marilee comes back. She doesn't look nearly as tired as she did when she left the room and I wonder why until she says, "Lizabett, you have company."

Marilee nods her head toward the main part of the diner. "It's that fireman, Jake Nelson. He's asking for you."

"Oh." He's the last thing on my mind.

I see Quinn and Rick look at each other, though, and I realize I have no choice but to go talk to Jake if I want it to be clear that I can make my own decisions about the men I want to date. Right now, the whole thing doesn't seem so important, but it shouldn't take more than a few minutes and Marilee is looking at me like she's expecting me to go out front. I remember how hard we used to try to maintain some semblance of a normal life in the midst of our cancer, so I know Marilee wants me to talk to Jake and not hold back because I'm worried about her.

I leave the Sisterhood room and see Jake Nelson standing beside the counter in the main dining area and looking nervous.

"Hi," I say as I walk over to him.

"Thanks for coming out," Jake says with a nod. "I didn't know your friend just got back from the doctor's until the waitress told me."

I nod. That would have been Shelley. She'd been in the Sisterhood room a few times asking for news, and I know Marilee would have given her an update.

"I hope everything is okay," Jake says.

"Marilee doesn't really know anything yet," I say. "But the doctor said the odds are good. She'll know more in a couple of days."

Jake nods. "I came to ask you to go out to dinner with me, but I can tell this isn't a good time. I can wait and ask later. That is, if you want to go."

I look at Jake. He is a handsome man. His black hair is thick, and his smile is infectious. He genuinely looks concerned about Marilee, so that counts in his favor. Any woman should be happy to date him.

"I'm not sure I can do dinner, but I'd love to have lunch with you—if that would work," I say. "Maybe right here at the Pews?"

Jake's smile turns to a full-blown grin. "That would be great. How about tomorrow?"

"Fine," I say.

Jake doesn't stay long after we make our plans, which is just as well because I had been fighting the urge to sigh the whole time I was talking to him. I couldn't help but think back to that day when I went to kindergarten because my mother told me I had to carry on with my life even though I felt like staying home. A date shouldn't seem like a duty.

When Jake is gone, I go back into the Sisterhood room. Everyone looks up when I enter, but no one asks me what Jake wanted. Both Rick and Quinn are looking a little grim, but they are silent. I know the questions are going to spill out from the sisters the minute we are alone. Quinn doesn't look like he'll leave Marilee anytime soon, though, and I figure the sisters can ask me their questions tomorrow evening at our regular meeting. It might even be nice to have something to talk about instead of Marilee's test results, which probably won't be back by then anyway.

Becca and I leave together and Carly goes back to work. It's almost five o'clock, and the after-work crowd is going to flood the Pews in a half hour, so Uncle Lou will be glad for her help.

I figure Quinn will spend some more time talking with Marilee, and Rick will go back to the fire station. I plan to start reading the other book on prayer that I have at home. I'd like to learn more about praying with other people. I'll take a few minutes and describe the feelings I had earlier for the journal as well. I'm beginning to wonder how powerful the Sisterhood would have been if we'd known about God and prayer sooner.

Chapter Fourteen

❦

"One cannot collect all the beautiful shells on the beach."

— Anne Morrow Lindbergh

Marilee is the one who brought us this quote about shells. She and her mother had gone to the Sea of Cortez and wandered on the beach there, looking at all of the seashells that washed to shore. She wasn't supposed to, but Marilee brought us each back a tiny shell. That was one of those rare meetings when we didn't mention cancer once in the whole evening. It was wonderful just looking at those gems from the sea.

I feel like we have those seashells back in our hands. We are finished with the silent knitting time of our Sisterhood meeting, and, after we asked Marilee if she had heard anything and she said no, we stopped talking about cancer. We learned years ago how to escape our worries, and we have something even better than the seashells tonight. We have that wedding dress.

When Uncle Lou brought in our usual pot of tea, he asked Carly if she could help him with something in the kitchen. Marilee looked a little puzzled by the request, but she didn't say anything as Carly stood up and followed Uncle Lou out of the Sisterhood room.

"How was your date?" Marilee asked me after the door closed behind Carly.

"It was quick," I say. "Jake had to get back to the fire station, so he couldn't stay long."

I don't mention that Jake brought a note from Rick announcing that he had confirmed a place for the wedding and he'd tell me all about it tonight. I'm relieved that we finally have a place. Rick had already told Becca to put a notice on the Web site for the wedding asking people to gather at the Pews for final directions to the location of the ceremony. Becca said that people were getting into what she called the surprise wedding location.

Marilee doesn't have more time to ask about my lunch with Jake because Carly opens the French doors and comes back into the room carrying the big white box.

"What's that?" Marilee asks, her voice breathless like she might suspect what it is but is afraid to assume.

"It's your wedding dress," I say as Carly dramatically opens the box and pulls the gown out enough so that Marilee can see it. The overhead light makes the pearls on the cream-colored satin shimmer with a soft glow.

"But how?" Marilee looks at the dress in bewilderment.

"It's Lizabett's doing," Becca says from where she's been sitting.

Marilee comes over and gives me a hug even though I'm still sitting in my chair and can't really reach up to hug her back.

"I can't believe it. How did you ever get something so beautiful?" she asks.

I stand up so I can hug her back. "Rick and I pulled it off. I made the arrangements, and Rick got the guys at work to help."

After Marilee wipes a few tears away, she goes over to touch the dress. By now Carly has it completely out of the box and we can all see that the dress is beautiful.

"You got me a Vera Wang?" Marilee asks in astonishment as she lifts the dress up and sees the tag inside.

I nod, my happiness spilling out of me. "You're only getting married once. We wanted it to be your dream wedding—at least as much as is possible."

Marilee sets the dress back into the box, and it's a good thing because she's crying in earnest now. The rest of the sisters draw close and give her one of our special group hugs.

"I thought we could meet tomorrow and talk about hairstyles," Carly says once we've finished the hug and separated again. Her excitement is quiet, but it makes her voice rich. "There's a veil on the bottom of this box, and we'll want to plan how you want to wear your hair to show it the best."

"And we'll need to see about shoes, unless you have some in your closet," Becca says. She's getting in to it, too. "That's my department."

"I just can't believe it," Marilee says as she looks at each of us.

"Well, believe it, because you're having a wedding," Becca says with a grin.

Just then, Uncle Lou opens the French doors. He has the diner's phone in one hand.

"It's for you," he says to Marilee as he holds out the phone. "A Dr. Wells or Walls or—"

"Dr. Walsh," Marilee says with a quick intake of breath. Her face goes pale.

Uncle Lou nods. "That sounds right."

The sisters all look at each other. I can see fear on everyone's face.

"Just because he called when he's not on duty doesn't mean there's a problem," Becca finally says.

Marilee nods. "You're right."

I should step outside to call Quinn on my cell phone, but I can't make myself move. *Oh God, please, please, please.* I automatically reach into my pocket looking for something and stop myself—the Lizzie stone won't help any of us. Instead, I put out my hand and Carly takes it. We squeeze each other's fingers.

Marilee's face is stony. I can tell it takes courage for her to take the phone from Uncle Lou, but she does. For a moment, she just holds the phone to her ear.

"Hello," she finally says. "Dr. Walsh?"

I watch as the color returns to Marilee's face. She's listening to the doctor, and her lips start to move until she's smiling.

"You're sure?" she says into the phone. By now Marilee is looking at us as well. I can see by her eyes that the news she's hearing is good. Carly and I relax our grip on each other's hands.

"Thank you for calling," Marilee says as she pushes

the Off button on the phone and sets it down on the table. She looks around at us, and her eyes are sparkling. "He says I'm fine. I have something called a fibroadenoma—it's just tissue. It's not cancer at all. He says we should remove it, but it's just a small operation and—oh, I've got to call Quinn."

I need to sit down. Marilee walks out of the Sisterhood room, dialing Quinn's phone number as she goes. I know she'll want to tell Uncle Lou and her mother right away, too. I look over at the rest of the sisters. They look as spent as I feel.

"Thank God," Becca says as she sits down in a chair next to me.

"Amen," Carly says as she takes the other chair.

We just look at each other for a moment.

"I can't believe it," I finally say. Usually, when I worry about something, it happens. I know I'm not supposed to think that God or the Universe or Whoever causes something bad to happen when I'm too happy, but that has been what I've thought for so many years. "It's really going to be okay."

"Yeah." Becca nods.

I feel like I'm free. And my spine is tingling a little. All of the physical reactions I thought would come upon me when I walked up that church aisle and pledged myself to God are happening now.

"I should write it down in the journal," I finally say as I reach behind me for my knitting bag. "Not that I know the words to describe it."

"I do," Becca says.

I hand her the journal when I pull it out of my bag. She takes a pen out of her purse and, before I know it, is writing in the journal.

* * *

This is Becca. Today our friend and sister Marilee was told she is free of cancer. I can only praise God for this. I know that she would have accepted God's will in this, no matter what He wanted. I also know that sickness, like health, can bring glory to Him. But I am so very happy that He continues to keep Marilee free of cancer. Now, when she promises to love Quinn in sickness and health, she can hope for many years together to do that.

When Becca gives the journal back to me, I read what she has written.

"That's beautiful." I stand up and put the journal back in my bag.

"I figure their wedding day will be really happy now," Becca says as she stretches and stands up herself. "I'm glad you got that dress for them. I think they'll want to celebrate."

"I couldn't have done it without Rick and the guys at the station," I say. Looking at Becca and Carly, I notice how tired they both look. I doubt any of us have slept much in the past few nights.

"I think we should make it an early night," I say. "Marilee's going to be on the phone for hours."

Carly nods. "Sounds good to me."

We walk out of the Sisterhood room together. We see Marilee sitting at one of the side tables in the main part of the diner. She is talking on the phone to someone, so we wave as we walk toward the door. She smiles back and whispers my brother's name to us.

The air is cool on the sidewalk outside of the Pews and we stop a minute to pull our sweaters closer to us.

Becca is parked in a different structure than Carly and I, so we say good-night to her and begin the walk down the street.

"Quinn must be working tonight," Carly says as we come to the old fire station.

I nod. "I can't think of anything else that would keep him from hanging up the phone and driving over to be with Marilee."

Just then we see a figure come out of the side door of the old fire station. Even in the dark, I can tell it is my brother. He has his cell phone to his ear, and he's got his regular clothes on instead of his firemen gear, so I figure he was given permission to leave work early tonight.

He's so intent on his phone conversation that he doesn't even notice Carly and I are on the street along with a dozen other people who are passing by. I don't say anything until he's walked by, but then I turn to Carly.

"I think I envy my brother," I say with a smile.

"Your day will come," she replies.

I nod even though I'm not sure if I agree or not.

Carly and I go separate ways in the parking structure, and I drive home. I know one thing I'm going to do when I get there. Now that God has answered our prayers for Marilee, I am starting to feel really disloyal that I have my old Lizzie stone sitting on my nightstand at home. It's not that I'm keeping the stone, exactly; it's just that I haven't thought of what to do with it. That needs to change, though. It's time I put that old stone out of my life. And there's no time like tonight.

For some reason, I'm not surprised when I see Rick

sitting on the top step of my mother's porch. I park my car on the street and walk up the sidewalk to the house.

"You heard?" I say when I get close enough.

He nods. "One of the guys from the station called me."

"So you're waiting up for Quinn?" I sit on the step next to him. "I'm not sure when he'll be home."

Rick is quiet, and I hear the rustle of the wild parrots in the trees beside us.

"I was waiting for you," he finally says.

"Oh." My heart skips a beat.

And then he continues, "There's some things about the wedding we need to go over."

"Of course," I say. Being friends with Rick is going to take some getting used to, and I'm not sure I'll be able to handle it. Maybe after the wedding I'll find a place of my own again. If I'm not living right next door, I don't think he will be so intent on being friends.

"I found a violinist today. Pastor Engstrom knows an older man who used to play some professionally. I mentioned him to Quinn, and he thought the guy would be just what Marilee would want. He even has a tuxedo he can wear." Rick grins at me. "I know how you like those tuxedoes."

"I hope you have the ones for you and Quinn rented."

"I pick them up on Saturday," Rick says as he pulls a small notebook out of his jacket pocket. "I've got the list you gave me over the phone right here."

"Marilee is going to be so happy," I say. "And the upstairs of the old fire station is a perfect place to have it."

I should have thought of it myself. The wood floors have been polished so often they have a deep, elegant gleam. And the rustic brick walls and high-beamed ceiling will be a natural for the occasion.

"We make a good team—you and me," Rick says, and I hear the satisfaction in his voice. "One of the guys down at the station was even saying we should get this wedding written up in one of those bridal magazines. How many couples get married in a fire station?"

"None that I know of," I say. "And we'll have to take pictures." I look down at the list I gave Rick. "Oh, I see you've already checked that off."

"Like I said, we make a good team," Rick says. "I wouldn't have a clue what to do without your list."

"Great," I say. I know I did most of the planning, but I didn't really expect to have so much help from Rick. He organized the other firefighters and my brothers to help.

"I haven't told Marilee or Quinn about the arrangements," Rick says. "I thought I'd let you decide if you want it to be a surprise."

"I don't know that it needs to be a surprise, but I just don't think we need to worry them with the details. I know they want to just savor the fact that Marilee is well."

"That's what I thought, too," Rick says.

Rick slips his notebook back into his pocket and we sit in silence on the porch for a while. I hear some soft cooing coming from the wild parrots and I wonder if there are a couple of birds in love up in the trees.

After a bit, Rick stands up and then bends down to give me a kiss on my head again. I hope the parrots don't see him giving me such a brotherly kiss; it's enough to discourage romance in any species.

After Rick leaves, I walk into the house and go upstairs to my bedroom. I notice my rose is almost wilted. I'll need to throw it out tomorrow. I wonder if I should bury the rose and my Lizzie stone in the backyard. They were both gifts from Rick, and neither one of them meant what I'd hoped they did.

Chapter Fifteen

"What is drama but life with the dull bits cut out."
—Alfred Hitchcock

I was the one who brought this quote to the Sisterhood meeting the first fall we met. And it wasn't just because we had that whole Hitchcock thing going. For some reason, I was convinced that Carly could become a famous actress, and I wanted to encourage her in that direction. She wasn't moved by my vision, though.

Later I realized that the reason the rest of us were all so determined to do such hard things—me with my ballet, Becca with her law school and Marilee with transforming her uncle's diner—was because we felt we had to squeeze the rest of our lives into just a few months. We had no time for the small, ordinary dreams of other kids our age.

Carly was different, though. She always managed to live life with just the right balance in her dreams. I never knew how she did that.

* * *

Friday goes by in a whirl, and Saturday is here before I'm ready. The one thing we hadn't thought about earlier was the need for bridesmaid dresses, and I had to work with Carly for the better part of the day yesterday collecting fancy ball gowns from the closets of her aunt's friends. Carly might have moved out of San Marino a year ago, but her aunt still lives there and attends the kind of functions that show off elegant gowns. Carly knows how to move in those circles, so she talks to the women while I just stand there wondering how people can have that many ball gowns.

Once we got the dresses, Carly and I took them to an express dry cleaner who promised to have them ready by two o'clock today. And then, of course, I needed to pick up the cake and talk to Uncle Lou about the appetizers he's providing and—

Before I know it Saturday evening is here and Becca, Carly and I are standing in our very own room at the Pews. We are swishing around in long, full-skirted gowns in different shades of pink. My fuchsia dress even has a little pocket in the side seam. I figured the pocket was there for a purpose, and I put the Lizzie stone in it earlier. I am determined to get rid of that thing tonight at last.

In the meantime, I admire the small pink and white rose bouquets sitting on the table waiting for us. There are so many different colors of pink in the roses that it makes the various colors in our dresses look planned. Rick assured me earlier that one of the firemen's wives had taken care of the flowers at the fire station so we would have roses everywhere.

I have been amazed at how eager everyone has been to help with this wedding. Quinn lined up the flower girls that I had talked to Marilee about earlier.

"They're here," Becca announces. She's been looking out the French-door windows and waiting for Marilee and Quinn to come into the diner.

"I've got her dress ready," Carly says. Earlier, she put a high hook in the Sisterhood wall just so she could hang Marilee's dress there. She said we needed a wedding-dress wall.

"I'll get the covers for the windows," Becca says as she walks over to the shelves and picks up two light blankets that she brought to put over the French door windows.

Marilee is going to change into her dress in our room, and Quinn is going to change in Marilee's office down the hall. All of the guests will be arriving in a half hour, and then we'll all walk the half block down to the fire station together.

All of a sudden I am flooded with feelings about what an important turning point this is for Marilee and my brother.

"I'll be right back," I say as I open the French doors. "I just want to give my brother a hug before everything gets going."

I know Quinn will still be around; he's not moving out of town or anything. But things will change when he's married. I doubt he'll be over at Mom's cooking breakfast as often or sitting on the porch waiting for me to come home.

"Hey," I say when I get to the hallway and see Quinn reach for the doorknob of Marilee's office.

My brother turns around and smiles. "Hey, yourself."

The hallway is dimly lit and quiet. I walk up to my brother and put my arms out for a hug. "I'm going to miss you."

Quinn enfolds me in a hug. "I thought you'd be glad to get rid of your Old Mother Hen."

I look up at him and smile. "I know you meant well."

Quinn shakes his head. "I shouldn't have tried to protect you so much. Here you are, all grown up, and I'm still treating you like you're in high school."

"Well, there's always time to change."

Quinn nods. "From now on, I'm going to let you decide who you want to date."

I'm not sure my brother has it in him to not interfere at all. "Well, you can still give me your opinion. Just let me make the decision. Like with this guy, Jake—"

"I'm not talking about Jake," Quinn says.

My brother has a guilty look on his face. I wonder what he's done now. "Who are you talking about?"

I don't suppose it's good etiquette to snap at your brother on his wedding day.

Quinn leans over and gives me a kiss on the top of my head. "You're going to have to ask Rick who I wouldn't let you date."

Then, before I can get my jaw to work, Quinn opens the door to Marilee's office and steps inside, leaving me in the hallway with a closed door in front of me. I suppose my brother and Rick have completely crushed some poor guy who wanted to ask me out. I know they mean well, but do they *see* lines of men out there waiting to date me? Before they chase everyone away, they should at least give me a chance.

I take a deep breath. I am not going to spend tonight

irritated with my brother. It's his wedding. I plan to enjoy every minute of it.

When I get back to the Sisterhood room, Marilee already has her dress on.

"Wow," I say when I slip in the door.

"Isn't she beautiful?" Carly says.

I can only nod. Someone dimmed the overhead light, and it makes the pearls in Marilee's dress shine. The pearls aren't even the most amazing thing, though. Marilee's face is pink, and it radiates happiness.

"Just one last thing," Becca says as she lifts up the headpiece for the veil and tucks it into Marilee's hair. Delicate cream-colored lace flows down Marilee's back as Becca clips the headpiece in place.

"You're sure you don't want to know where we're taking you?" I ask. Earlier, Marilee had said she didn't want to know the location of her wedding.

She shakes her head. "Just get me there so I can say my I do's."

We have too many skirts to do a group hug like we usually do, but we still stand in a circle and hold hands.

"I've never had better friends," Marilee says as she looks at each of us slowly, one by one.

I'm blinking back tears and am afraid to look at the others because they're probably trying not to cry, too.

We're silent for a moment, and then Becca finally says, "Well, what are we waiting for? We've got a wedding to go to."

We go out into the main part of the Pews, and I see that all sixty of the guests are waiting. I see Marilee's parents and my mother. Uncle Lou is standing to the side in his best suit. There's a sign on the diner that the

Pews is closed for a family event tonight. It is dark outside, but I see a yellow glow coming through the windows.

Then Rick opens the door to the outside and suddenly the guests move to either side of the door, forming an aisle. Two men in suits come through the door carrying a roll of red carpet. They bend down and roll the carpet out so that Marilee can walk down it.

"Oh," Marilee breathes out in wonder.

Before I know it, my brother is there in his tuxedo to escort his bride down the aisle and outside.

The bridesmaids follow Marilee and Quinn out of the diner, and we see how Cinderella is going to the ball. The man who owns the horse and carriage is waiting outside the door. Rose garlands hang from the horse, and I know the flowers are real because I can smell them. The carriage driver is wearing a tuxedo and looks regal as he holds the horse in place while Marilee and Quinn step up into a velvet-draped buggy.

After the wedding couple is settled, I look around me. This block of Colorado Boulevard has been blocked off, and I see firemen standing and holding old-fashioned lanterns all the way between the diner and the historic fire station. The sound of a violin comes my way, and I see a man starting to walk beside the carriage and play a love song.

There's a full moon in the sky, and the sight of the guests beginning to follow the buggy down the street makes me blink back a tear.

"Here," someone says, and I look up to see Rick holding out a pressed white handkerchief.

"Where'd you get that?" I mumble as I take it.

"With the tux," he says with a grin. "I wondered what it was for, but now I know. Women and weddings."

"Well, who wouldn't cry?" I say as I dab at my eyes. "It's beautiful."

Truthfully, I don't know what part of the scene I'm describing. I have never seen Rick look like this. The light of the lanterns makes his eyes smolder. And the shadows make his jaw forceful. I can see why tuxedoes are popular for weddings. They make a man seem so very romantic.

"We don't want to be late," Rick says and holds his elbow out so he can escort me.

I'm speechless as I take his arm. I do know, though, that Cinderella missed out on a lot when she took a carriage to her ball. There's nothing like walking with a prince on a moonlit night with the soft sounds of a violin in the air.

Unfortunately, Rick and I had to part when we got to the fire station.

"Meet you under the bulb," Rick says with a wink before I start to climb up the stairs to the top floor.

Someone has transformed the top floor of the station into a fantasy wonderland. Pink balloons with silver streamers float in the rafters. The red carpet has been rolled out again, leading to a spot in the middle of the floor right next to the brass fire pole. Chairs are lined up on either side of the carpet and people are starting to take their seats.

Quinn walks up to the top of the carpet aisle where Pastor Engstrom is now standing. Marilee waits in the back. I go to stand beside her.

"I can't believe it," she says to me in a whisper. "How did you do all of this?"

"Everyone helped. Rick and the other firemen did a lot of it."

I see Rick take his place beside Quinn.

Just then the violinist starts to play again, and three little girls holding baskets and wearing pink dresses come giggling up the stairs. Rick gives the girls a cue and they start slowly walking up the aisle throwing rose petals everywhere.

"Flower girls," Marilee says. "Just like we wanted."

The rest of the ceremony floats by like a dream. Becca, Carly and I walk forward and stand at the front while Marilee walks down the aisle.

Pastor Engstrom talks about commitment and manages to make a reference or two about the lightbulb that is hanging over the bridal couple's head. I notice a few flashes go off when the pastor points up at the lightbulb and says it's a reminder to all of us that we need to be faithful.

I look over during the vows and see Rick standing beside Quinn and glancing at me. He seems a little guilty and looks away once he sees me. I suddenly realize that Rick is using the wedding to get ready for the lightbulb ceremony. I twist my head a little and see a woman who looks like she's taking notes. I bet she's a reporter.

Then I look back at the joy on Marilee's face and decide it doesn't matter if there's some publicity happening here. Before long, I'm drawn back into the ceremony.

When Quinn kisses his bride, I can't help being a little bit jealous. I look over at Rick again; I am tired of being kissed on the top of my head by a man who considers me his sister.

When Pastor Engstrom pronounces Quinn and Marilee husband and wife, though, all my jealousy leaves me; I am filled with joy for them. The violinist starts to play a happy tune, and Quinn leads Marilee down the aisle. This time everyone is throwing rose petals.

While Quinn and Marilee shake hands with their guests, the firemen lift linens off of tables on the other side of the room. Uncle Lou made dozens of crab-stuffed mushrooms earlier today along with miniature quiches and large grilled shrimp, and they're all now in view. Sparkling cider is being passed around in crystal glasses, and by the time the newlyweds are finished shaking hands, the reception has begun.

I sit for a bit on the sidelines just listening to the joy in Marilee's voice as she talks with her other guests. There's something about a wedding that promises a new life, and it reminds me of the changes I need to make in my life.

The skirt on my dress is so full that I almost forgot I have the Lizzie stone with me, but now that the reception is going strong I know I can leave for a little bit and take care of that stone. It's time to let it go. I still can't just throw it in the trash, though.

I fix my eyes on the back of Rick's head, and, sure enough, he eventually turns around and begins to walk over to me.

"I think things are going pretty good, don't you?" he says when he sits down next to me.

"Everything is wonderful," I say. "But I need a favor."

Rick agrees to come with me, and I lead him down

the stairs and out the back door of the fire station. There's a small area in back of the station that is just big enough for a few benches and a couple of trees. Because we came out the back door, we don't see any street lights. A soft glow comes down from the windows above us, though.

I reach into my pocket and pull out the Lizzie stone. "Why did you have this in your pocket that day you gave it to me?"

Rick peers down at my hand. "Is that your Lizzie stone?"

I nod my head. "It's time for me to let it go, so I thought I'd have you complete the cycle—whatever you would have done with the stone if you hadn't given it to me—I'd like you to do it now."

Rick reaches over and takes the stone from my hand. Then he takes aim at the farthest tree and lets the stone fly. "I was practicing my aim in those days. For pitching."

I feel lighter now that I don't have that stone in my life, even though it didn't really weigh very much. Getting rid of old habits is liberating, so I decide to go one step further.

"I had a chat with Quinn a little bit ago," I begin.

After Rick finished his throw, he moved back close to me. "And?"

"He kind of apologized for being such an Old Mother Hen." That should be enough to give Rick the hint that he shouldn't follow in my brother's footsteps. "He said there was some guy you and he had warned off and that I should ask about him."

"He said that?"

I nod. "I know it's because you both care, but I'm old enough to—"

"It was me," Rick says.

Oh. All of a sudden, I wish I had a lightbulb close by. I can't see Rick's eyes in the darkness, and I don't know what he means. Does he mean he was the one who warned the other guy off or—

"I'm the guy Quinn didn't want you to date."

"But—" I don't understand this at all.

"I knew you wouldn't go out with me if Quinn objected," Rick says softly. "It took me a whole year to get him to agree to that first date."

"You've wanted to go out with me for a year?" My voice squeaks.

Rick gives a soft chuckle. "I've wanted to go out with you since that day I helped you with your ballet moves."

"But that's—" I can't add or subtract right now, so I have no idea how many years ago that was. All I know is that it was a lifetime.

"Are you okay?" Rick says as he puts out a hand to steady me. "I'm sure this comes as a surprise. That's one reason why I agreed with Quinn to wait. I figured you would want to take it slow."

"Slow?" I find my voice. "I proposed to you when I was seven years old. Does that sound like I wanted to take it *slow?*"

Rick's chuckle is warm, and I let it surround us. It makes my heart glad.

"Well, maybe I miscalculated some," Rick says as he reaches out his hand and traces the line of my jaw.

I shiver, and it's not because I'm cold. His chuckle fades, and his eyes smolder in the darkness. I couldn't look away from him now if I wanted to. Upstairs the violinist is starting to play again. I think the whole universe is full of music.

Then Rick bends his head and kisses me, fully and completely, on the lips.

I'm a little breathless when he pulls back. He looks a little shaken, too.

All I can think of is one thing, though.

"Never *ever* kiss me on the forehead again," I whisper a little fiercely.

Rick grins. "It's a deal."

Then he kisses me again.

Epilogue

Five Years Later

"I think it's a little dimmer," Marilee says. She's looking straight up at the lightbulb that is almost ready to celebrate its one hundred and tenth birthday. It's the middle of the afternoon and we're all taking a break from last-minute wedding preparations.

"It's going to burn out sometime," Quinn says. He's standing next to Marilee with his arm around her shoulders. If anyone asked him, he'd claim he was just being romantic, but I know my brother. He's got his arm there to keep her steady; she's six months pregnant, and he'll always be someone's Old Mother Hen.

"Well, it can't burn out today," Becca says confidently and then looks at the rest of us in sudden panic. "Can it? Please, tell me it can't."

Becca's dark hair is a mass of curls that sweep back from her face. She had her hair fixed special because she's going to be married this evening wearing an ivory lace veil that has been in Mark Russo's family for generations. His grandmother asked her to wear it when she welcomed Becca into their family. I know it means a lot to Becca. She's more nervous today than she was last month when she had her first court case as a new lawyer.

"I'm sure the lightbulb will cooperate," I say with a smile as I put my hand on Becca's arm. "And if it doesn't, that's okay, too."

Becca gives a slight snort. "Easy for you to say. You don't have four generations of the Russo family showing up here expecting to see it shining away. Besides, you've already been married under the thing." She looks back up at the old lightbulb and frowns. "I don't know why we decided to all have our weddings here. I know we wanted a tradition, but—"

"Since it's a historic place, it'll make up for us daring to wear those black bridesmaid dresses," I tease. The dresses are hanging on the wedding wall back at the Pews. Becca wants to do the grand march down Colorado Boulevard, too, so we'll get dressed there.

She smiles a little at me. "Hey, black isn't always about grief. It's also about class. Besides, those dresses are going to look great in here. Even Grandma Russo will approve."

I have to agree with Becca. We sisters will all look sleek and sophisticated in our dresses, especially because the men will be in tuxedoes. The old fire station makes the perfect backdrop for this kind of elegance. The aged brick of the walls and the high windows are stately. This upper part of the old fire station has been rented out for many functions over the past few years. I have planned a good dozen weddings here myself. The fire station earns enough from renting out the space to keep the building open, and there's a plan to turn the bottom part into a museum next year.

"I still keep worrying about the bulb, though," Becca says as she looks at me. "What if it goes out tonight?"

I'm Becca's wedding-planner, and I've learned how to calm the nerves of brides, but just then Mark and Rick finish walking up the stairs. They must have heard the conversation, because Mark doesn't miss a beat.

"I don't care if all the lights in Los Angeles burn out tonight—we're getting married," Mark says as he walks over to Becca. He's tall enough that, when he wraps his arms around her, her face rests against his shoulder. The man might be worth millions, but I don't think Becca cares about that at all. I can see her relax into him.

"I guess we could always use candles if we need," Becca mutters.

"I'll put up a torch if we have to," Mark agrees.

I don't have much time to notice how close Mark is holding Becca because Rick is soon holding me just as close.

"Aren't you glad we didn't wait five years to get married?" Rick whispers in my ear. "We would have had years to be that kind of nervous."

I feel the solid weight of him next to me, and he smells good. "I might have never made it," I say contentedly. I love having Rick's arms around me.

He's right. We didn't have long to worry about our wedding. The two of us got married six months after Quinn and Marilee did. I expected the other sisters to say we were being impulsive, but they seemed to understand. After all, it wasn't so impulsive considering we'd first discussed getting married seventeen years ago, even if we were underage at the time.

When Rick and I opted to get married at the old fire station like Quinn and Marilee, a tradition was born for the Sisterhood. Rick and I held hands and said our vows under this same lightbulb. Carly and Randy did the same when they married a year later.

The bulb became a symbol of steadfast commitment to all of us. We talked about it often enough in the Sisterhood journal that Carly finally drew an illustration of it for the cover.

We didn't plan it, but the lightbulb eventually became a symbol for teenagers with cancer. One of the reporters writing about the lightbulb mentioned we had used it on the cover of the journal we were keeping about our struggle to take our lives back after cancer. Nurses from several local hospitals asked to have copies of our journal for some of their cancer patients. We have a Web site now for the journal, and we've been getting some tender notes from young women telling us how they feel about illness and friendship. We give the notes to our old counselor, Rose, and she's starting some more groups.

As I stand here in Rick's arms, with my sisters and their chosen men nearby, I feel like we have come full circle. I'm not surprised when Becca calls for a group hug.

The eight of us gather around in a close huddle, and, as has become our habit, we take turns showering blessings upon each other.

Like always, Quinn ends it with, "And God bless us, each and everyone."

As we pull away slightly, Rick gives me a squeeze around my waist.

"God's already blessed me with you," he whispers in my ear and then gives me a quick kiss on my lips.

"Amen to that." I grin and give him a kiss right back.

* * * * *

Dear Reader,

This is the last of the Sisterhood of the Dropped Stitches books, and I want to thank you for sharing in the lives of these four friends. The books have taken us on quite a journey—from a home for troubled teenagers in Hollywood, to a diner in Old Town Pasadena and then to a fabulous wedding in a unique fire station. The thread that has tied everything together has been the friendship of these young women, who have faced life, and the possibility of death, together.

Everyone wants friends—the more the merrier. Unfortunately, we don't always take time to become close friends. Getting to know someone else deeply takes time.

Some of the most practical advice in *Proverbs* is in 18:24: "A man who hath friends must show himself friendly." The friends in my own life have proven the truth of this statement. I hope that you have good friends, but if you do not, take to heart the advice in *Proverbs,* and that might change.

I love to hear from my readers. If you get a chance, visit my Web site at www.JanetTronstad.com and send me an e-mail. If you don't have access to a computer, you can always drop me a note in care of the editors at Steeple Hill, 233 Broadway, Suite 1001, New York, New York, 10279.

Sincerely yours,

Janet Tronstad

QUESTIONS FOR DISCUSSION

1. In the beginning of the book, Lizabett is getting ready to make an announcement that she has decided to become a Christian. How did she feel about telling her friends? How would you feel in her place? How have you felt when you've told someone close to you about your faith?

2. When Lizabett remembers her childhood, she recalls going to kindergarten for the first time. She was scared, and her friend Rick gave her a stone to hold, telling her it would make things okay. Have you ever been given something like that to ease your fears? Tell us about it. Do you think it was the right thing for Rick to do?

3. If you could talk to Lizabett about her Lizzie stone, what would you say? Have you ever had something similar in your life (good-luck charm, etc.)?

4. Lizabett and Rick have been friends for many years. Over the years, the way they felt about each other changed. Have you had a friendship that has changed over the years? How did it change?

5. Lizabett had wanted to be a ballerina since she was a little girl. And then she got cancer in the muscles of her leg. She could still dance, but it was never the same. Have you ever had something happen that made one of your dreams difficult? What did you do about it?

6. Lizabett's brother, Quinn, has felt responsible for her since their father died when they were young. How do you think that would shape a person's life? Have you ever had responsibilities thrust upon you that were not yours? How did you deal with it?

7. The lightbulb in the book is a real lightbulb. Reread the dedication to this book. Do you have any thoughts on this lightbulb?

8. When Marilee has a mammogram that scares her, what does she do? Do you ever hide away from people when you're scared of something?

9. Marilee calls off her wedding to Quinn because she doesn't want him to go through bad times with her. If you could talk to Marilee, what would you advise her to do? Are there times when you should spare your spouse worry about something related to your medical condition?

10. Marilee is willing to give up her dream wedding to marry Quinn. What are some things you have given up for love of a spouse, friend or child?

11. At the end of the book, all of the sisters are married. If you are married, think back to your own wedding day. What things turned out differently than you had thought they would when you said your vows?

*Turn the page for a sneak preview of
bestselling author Jillian Hart's novella,
"Finally a Family"*

*One of two heartwarming stories
celebrating motherhood in
IN A MOTHER'S ARMS.*

*On sale April 2009, only from
Steeple Hill Love Inspired Historical.*

Chapter One

Montana Territory, 1884

Molly McKaslin sat in her rocking chair in her cozy little shanty with her favorite book in hand. The lush new-spring green of the Montana prairie spread out before her like a painting, framed by the wooden window. The blue sky was without a single cloud to mar it. Lemony sunshine spilled over the land and across the open window's sill. The door was wedged open, letting the outside noises in—the snap of laundry on the clothes line and the chomping crunch of an animal grazing. My, it sounded terribly close.

The peaceful afternoon quiet shattered with a crash. She leaped to her feet to see her good—and only—china vase splintered on the newly washed wood floor. She stared in shock at the culprit standing at her other window. A golden cow with a white blaze down her face poked her head further across the sill. The bovine gave a woeful moo. One look told her this was the only animal in the yard.

"And just what are you doing out on your own?" She set her book aside.

The cow lowed again. She was a small heifer, still probably more baby than adult. The cow lunged against the sill, straining toward the cookie racks on the table.

"At least I know how to catch you." She grabbed a cookie off the rack and the heifer's eyes widened. "I don't recognize you, so I don't think you belong here."

Molly skirted around the mess on the floor and headed toward the door. This was the consequence of agreeing to live in the country, when she had vowed never to do so again. But her path had led her to this opportunity, living on her cousin's land and helping the family. God had quite a sense of humor, indeed.

Before she could take two steps into the soft, lush grass surrounding her shanty, the cow came running, head down, big brown eyes fastened on the cookie. The ground shook.

Uh oh. Molly's heart skipped two beats.

"No, Sukie, no!" High, girlish voices carried on the wind.

Molly briefly caught sight of two identical school-aged girls racing down the long dirt road. The animal was too single-minded to respond. She pounded the final few yards, her gaze fixed on the cookie.

"Stop, Sukie. Whoa." Molly kept her voice low and kindly firm. She knew cows responded to kindness better than to anything else. She also knew they were not good at stopping, so she dropped the cookie on the ground and neatly stepped out of the way. The cow skidded well past the cookie and the place where Molly had been standing.

"It's right here." She showed the cow where the oatmeal treat was resting in the clean grass. While the animal backed up and nipped up the goody, Molly grabbed the cow's rope halter.

"Good. She didn't stomp you into bits." One of the girls said in serious relief. "She ran me over real good just last week."

"We thought you were a goner," the second girl said. "She's real nice, but she doesn't see very well."

"She sees well enough to have found me." Molly studied the girls. They both had identical black braids and golden-hazel eyes and fine-boned porcelain faces. One twin wore a green calico dress with matching sun-bonnet, while the other wore blue. She recognized the girls from church and around town. " Aren't you the doctor's children?"

"Yep, that's us." The first girl offered a beaming, dimpled smile. "I'm Penelope and that's Prudence. We're real glad you found Sukie."

"We wouldn't want a cougar to get her."

"Or a bear."

What adorable children. A faint scattering of freckles dappled across their sun-kissed noses, and there was glint of trouble in their eyes as the twins looked at one another. The place in her soul thirsty for a child of her own ached painfully. She felt hollow and empty, as if her body would always remember carrying the baby she had lost. For one moment it was as if the wind died and the earth vanished.

"Hey, what is she eating?" One of the girls tumbled forward. "It smells like a cookie. You are a bad girl, Sukie."

"Did she walk into your house and eat off the counter?" Penelope wanted to know.

The grass crinkled beneath her feet as the cow tugged her toward the girls. "No, she went through the window."

Penelope went up on tiptoe. "I see them. They look real good."

Molly gazed down at their sweet and innocent faces. She wasn't fooled. Then again, she was a soft touch. "I'll see what I can do."

She headed back inside. "Do you girls need help getting the cow home?"

"No. She's real tame." Penelope and the cow trailed after her, hesitating outside the door. "We can lead her anywhere."

"Yeah, she only runs off when she's looking for us."

"Thank you so much, Mrs.—" Penelope took the napkin-wrapped stack of cookies. "We don't know your name."

"This is the McKaslin ranch," Prudence said thoughtfully. "But I know you're not Mrs. McKaslin."

"I'm the cousin. I moved here this last winter. You can call me Molly."

Penelope gave her twin a cookie. Beneath the brim of her sunbonnet, her face crinkled with serious thought. "You don't know our pa yet?"

"No, I only know Dr. Frost by reputation. I hear he's a fine doctor." That was all she knew. Of course she had seen his fancy black buggy speeding down the country roads at all hours. Sometimes she caught a brief sight of the man driving as the horse-drawn vehicle passed— an impression of a black Stetson, a strong granite profile and impressively wide shoulders.

Although she was on her own and free to marry, she paid little heed to eligible men. All she knew of Doctor

Sam Frost was that he was a widower and a father and a faithful man, for he often appeared very serious in church. She reached through the open door to where her coats hung on wall pegs and worked the sash off her winter wool.

Prudence smiled. "Our pa's real nice and you make good cookies."

"And you're real pretty." Penelope was so excited she didn't notice Sukie stealing her cookie. "Do you like Pa?"

"I don't know the man, so I can't like him. I suppose I can't dislike him either." She bent to secure the sash around Sukie's halter. "Let me walk you girls across the road."

"You ought to come home with us." Penelope grinned. "Then you can meet Pa."

"Do you want to get married?" Penelope's feet were planted.

So were Prudence's. "Yes! You could marry Pa. Do you want to?"

"M-marry your pa?" Shock splashed over her like icy water.

"Sure. You could be our ma."

"And then Pa wouldn't be so lonely anymore."

Molly blinked. The words were starting to sink in. The poor girls, wishing so much for a mother that they would take any stranger who was kind to them. "No, I certainly cannot marry a perfect stranger, but thank you for asking. I would take you two in a heartbeat."

"You would?" Penelope looked surprised. "Really?"

"We're an awful lot of trouble. Our housekeeper said that three times today since church."

"Does your pa know you propose on his behalf?"

"Now he does." A deep baritone answered. Dr. Frost marched into sight, rounding the corner of the shanty. His hat brim shaded his face, casting shadows across his chiseled features, giving him an even more imposing appearance. "Girls! Home! Not another word."

"But we had to save Sukie."

"She could have been eaten by a wolf."

Molly watched the good doctor's mouth twitch. She couldn't be sure, but a flash of humor could have twinkled in the depths of his eyes.

"You must be the cousin." He swept off his hat. The twinkle faded from his eyes and the hint of a grin from his lips. It was clear that while his daughters amused him, she did not. "I had no idea you would be so young."

"And pretty," Penelope, obviously the troublemaker, added mischievously.

Molly's face heated. The poor girl must need glasses. Although Molly was still young, time and sadness had made its mark on her. The imposing man had turned into granite as he faced her. Of course he had overheard his daughters' proposal, so that might explain it.

She smiled and took a step away from him. "Dr. Frost, I'm glad you found your daughters. I was about ready to bring them back to you."

"I'll save you the trouble." He didn't look happy. "Girls, take that cow home. I need to stay and apologize to Miss McKaslin."

She was a "Mrs." but she didn't correct him. She had put away her black dresses and her grief. Her marriage had mostly been a long string of broken dreams. She did better when she didn't remember. "Please don't be too hard on the girls on my behalf. Sukie's arrival livened up my day."

"At least there was no harm done." He winced. "There was harm? What happened?"

"I didn't say a word."

"No, but I could see it on your face."

Had he been watching her so closely? Or had she been so unguarded? Perhaps it was his closeness. She could see bronze flecks in his gold eyes, and smell the scents of soap and spring clinging to his shirt. A spark of awareness snapped within her like a candle newly lit. "It was a vase. Sukie knocked it off my windowsill when she tried to eat the flowers, but it was an accident."

"The girls should take better care of their pet." He drew his broad shoulders into an unyielding line. He turned to check on the twins, who were progressing down the road. The wind ruffled his dark hair. He seemed distant. Lost. "How much was the vase worth?"

How did she tell him it was without price? Perhaps it would be best not to open that door to her heart. "It was simply a vase."

"No, it was more." He stared at his hat clutched in both hands. "Was it a gift?"

"No, it was my mother's."

"And is she gone?"

"Yes."

"Then I cannot pay you its true value. I'm sorry." His gaze met hers with startling intimacy. Perhaps a door was open to his heart as well, because sadness tilted his eyes. He looked like a man with many regrets.

She knew well the weight of that burden. "Please, don't worry about it."

"The girls will replace it." His tone brooked no argument, but it wasn't harsh. "About what my daughters said to you."

"Do you mean their proposal? Don't worry. It's plain to see they are simply children longing for a mother's love."

"Thank you for understanding. Not many folks do."

"Maybe it's because I know something about longing. Life never turns out the way you plan it."

"No. Life can hand you more sorrow than you can carry." Although he did not move a muscle, he appeared changed. Stronger, somehow. Greater. "I'm sorry the girls troubled you, Miss McKaslin."

Mrs., but again she didn't correct him. It was the sorrow she carried that stopped her from it. She preferred to stand in the present with sunlight on her face. "It was a pleasure, Dr. Frost. What blessings you have in those girls."

"That I know." He tipped his hat to her, perhaps a nod of respect, and left her alone with the restless wind and the door still open in her heart.

* * * * *

Don't miss IN A MOTHER'S ARMS.
Featuring two brand-new novellas
from bestselling authors
Jillian Hart and Victoria Bylin.
Available April 2009
from Steeple Hill Love Inspired Historical.

And be sure to look for SPRING CREEK BRIDE
by Janice Thompson,
also available in April 2009.

Love Inspired

Everyone in Mule Hollow can see the resemblance between former Texas Ranger Zane Cantrell and Rose Vincent's son. Zane is in shock—how could Rose have kept such a secret from him? Rose reminds Zane that *he's* the one who walked away. Zane needs to convince her he had had no choice… and that's when the matchmaking begins.

Look for

Texas Ranger Dad

by

Debra Clopton

*Available April
wherever books are sold.*

REQUEST YOUR FREE BOOKS!

2 FREE INSPIRATIONAL NOVELS
PLUS 2
FREE
MYSTERY GIFTS

YES! Please send me 2 FREE Love Inspired® novels and my 2 FREE mystery gifts (gifts are worth about $10). After receiving them, if I don't wish to receive any more books, I can return the shipping statement marked "cancel". If I don't cancel, I will receive 4 brand-new novels every month and be billed just $4.24 per book in the U.S. or $4.74 per book in Canada, plus 25¢ shipping and handling per book and applicable taxes, if any*. That's a savings of over 20% off the cover price! I understand that accepting the 2 free books and gifts places me under no obligation to buy anything. I can always return a shipment and cancel at any time. Even if I never buy another book, the two free books and gifts are mine to keep forever.

113 IDN ERXA   313 IDN ERWX

Name	(PLEASE PRINT)	
Address		Apt. #
City	State/Prov.	Zip/Postal Code

Signature (if under 18, a parent or guardian must sign)

Order online at www.LoveInspiredBooks.com

Or mail to Steeple Hill Reader Service:

IN U.S.A.: P.O. Box 1867, Buffalo, NY 14240-1867
IN CANADA: P.O. Box 609, Fort Erie, Ontario L2A 5X3

Not valid to current subscribers of Love Inspired books.

Want to try two free books from another series?
Call 1-800-873-8635 or visit www.morefreebooks.com

* Terms and prices subject to change without notice. N.Y. residents add applicable sales tax. Canadian residents will be charged applicable provincial taxes and GST. Offer not valid in Quebec. This offer is limited to one order per household. All orders subject to approval. Credit or debit balances in a customer's account(s) may be offset by any other outstanding balance owed by or to the customer. Please allow 4 to 6 weeks for delivery. Offer available while quantities last.

Your Privacy: Steeple Hill Books is committed to protecting your privacy. Our Privacy Policy is available online at www.SteepleHill.com or upon request from the Reader Service. From time to time we make our lists of customers available to reputable third parties who may have a product or service of interest to you. If you would prefer we not share your name and address, please check here. ☐

LIREG08R

Love Inspired

TITLES AVAILABLE NEXT MONTH
Available March 31, 2009

TWICE UPON A TIME by Lois Richer
Weddings by Woodwards

Between his work and his twin boys, widower Reese Woodward has no time for love. Or so he thinks until he meets Olivia Hastings, his sister's best friend. Her past makes her wary of romance, but who can resist the adorable twins—or their father? Together they might find their second chance for a doubly blessed happy-ever-after.

TEXAS RANGER DAD by Debra Clopton
A Mule Hollow Novel

When Texas Ranger Zane Cantrell returns to Mule Hollow after years away, he comes face-to-face with the son of an old girlfriend—who also happens to be his son! Zane can't believe Rose Vincent kept this secret from him all these years. But he's eager to get to know his boy, and to prove he's never stopped loving Rose. Can they build a brand-new life together?

HOMECOMING BLESSINGS by Merrillee Whren

Small-town girl Amelia Hiatt and big-city businessman Peter Dalton think they have nothing in common. When they team up on a special project, they soon realize they're more alike than they could ever imagine. Except the big-city bachelor isn't ready to settle down, and Amelia is ready for a family of her own. But she's determined to change his mind—and his heart.

READY-MADE FAMILY by Cheryl Wyatt
Wings of Refuge

Ben Dillinger is used to playing the hero to damsels in distress, he's just not used to falling in love with them! When the pararescue jumper rescues single mom Amelia North and her daughter from a car accident, Ben realizes he's found the family he's been longing for. And he'll do whatever it takes to prove to her that he's the missing piece in her ready-made family.

LICNMBPA0309

side, reaching for the door. "Carter, stop!" He was the light of her life, leaving her. Panicked, she opened her mouth and screamed, *"Carter!"*

The heartrending sound, so unusual coming from her, stopped him. He raised his head wearing such a broken look that she couldn't move for another minute. But she had to keep him there, had to touch him, had to tell him all he meant to her. Forcing her legs into action, she ran toward the car.

Stopping directly before him, she raised a hand halfway to his face, wavered, mustered enough courage to graze his cheek with a finger before pulling back, then went with her own need and slipped her hand to the back of his neck. "I'm sorry," she tried to say, but the words were more mouthed than anything. "I'm sorry." She put her other hand flat on his chest, moved it up, finally slid it around his neck, went in close to him and managed a small sound against his throat. "I'm sorry, Carter, I'm sorry. I love you so much."

Carter stood very still for a long minute before slowly lifting his hands to her hips. "What?" he whispered hoarsely.

"I love you. Love you."

It was another long minute before he let out a breath, slid his arms around her and gathered her in.

Unable to help herself, Jessica began to cry. She could no more stop the tears than the words. "That was s-such a stupid thing for me to think of—and an insult t-to you. But something happened to me wh-when she said she'd known you before. Maybe I wanted to know what w-would happen—she's very attractive—but I l-love you so much—I don't know what I'd d-do if you ever left me."

He buried his face in her hair. Even muffled, his voice sounded rough. "You were pushing me away."

"I didn't know what else t-to do."

"You should have called me right away." He tightened his hold in a punishing way, and his voice remained gruff. "There's a solution, Jessica. There's always a solution. But you've got to keep your priorities straight. Top priority is us."

She knew that now. For as long as she lived, she'd never forget the sight of big, bad Carter Malloy with tears in his eyes. They had been tears of pain, and she'd put them there. They were humbling and horrifying. She never wanted to see them again.

Going up on tiptoe, she coiled her arms more tightly around his neck. "I love you," she whispered over and over again until finally he took her face in his hands and held her back.

"What do you want?" he whispered. His face was inches from hers, his thumbs brushing tears from under her glasses while his palms held her still. "Tell me."

"You. Just you."

"But what do you want?"

She knew that he needed to hear the words, and though they represented the ultimate exposure, she was ready for that, too. "I want to marry you. I want to take your name and use your credit cards and drive your car. I want to have your babies."

Carter didn't react, simply looked at her as though he weren't quite sure whether to believe her. So, clutching his wrists, she added, "I mean it. All of it. I think it's what I've wanted since the first time we made love, but I've been so afraid. You're so much more than me—"

"I'm not."

"You are. You've done so much more, come so much further in life, and that makes you so much more interesting. I want to marry you. I do, Carter. But if we got married and then you wanted out, I think I'd *die*, I love you so much."

"I won't want out," he said.

"But I didn't know that for sure until just now."

"I've been telling it to you for weeks."

"But I didn't know." She closed her eyes and whispered, "Oh, Carter, I don't ever want to lose you. Not ever."

"Then marry me. That's the first way to tie a man down."

Her eyes came open. "I'll marry you."

"And give me kids. That's the second way to tie a man down."

"Okay."

"And keep on teaching, because I'm so *proud* of what you do."

"You are?" she asked with a hesitant half smile.

"Damn it, yes," he said and crushed her to him. "I've always been proud of you. I'll always *be* proud of you— whether you're a scholar, mother of my kids, my wife or my woman."

Jessica smiled against his neck, feeling lighter and happier than she'd ever felt before. "I do love you," she whispered.

"Then trust me, too," he said. Taking her by the shoulders, he put her back a step and eyed her sternly. "Trust that I mean what I say when I tell you I love you. I don't want other women. I never *have* wanted other women the way I want you. I've never asked another woman to marry me, but I've asked you a dozen times. I *choose* you. I don't *have* to marry you. I *choose* you. I *want* to marry you."

"I get the point," she murmured, feeling a little shamefaced but delighted in spite of it.

"Do you also get the point about priorities?" he went on, and though a sternness remained in his voice, there was also an exciting vibrancy. "Crosslyn Rise is beautiful. It is venerable and stately and historic. I've got a whole lot of time invested in it, and money now, too, but if I had to choose between the Rise and you, there'd be no contest. I'd turn my back on the time, the money and the Rise just to have you. And I'd do it without a single regret." His eyes grew softer. "So I don't want you worrying about the zoning commission. We'll call Gordon and Gideon and the others. We'll work something out. But all that is secondary. Do you understand?"

"I do," she whispered, and it was true. In those few horrible minutes when she had seen his tears, when he had walked away from her and she'd had the briefest glimpse of the emptiness of life without him, Crosslyn Rise had been the last thing on her mind. Yes, the Rise was in trouble, but she could handle it. With Carter by her side, she could handle anything.

ARE YOU A ROMANCE READER WITH OPINIONS?

Openings are currently available for participation in the 1990-1991 Romance Reader Panel. We are looking for new participants from all regions of the country and from all age ranges.

If selected, you will be polled once a month by mail to comment on new books you have recently purchased, and may occasionally be asked for more in-depth comments. Individual responses will remain confidential and all postage will be prepaid.

Regular purchasers of one favorite series, as well as those who sample a variety of lines each month, are needed, so fill out and return this application today for more detailed information.

1. Please indicate the romance series you purchase from regularly at retail outlets.

Harlequin	Silhouette	
1. ☐ Romance	6. ☐ Romance	10. ☐ Bantam Loveswept
2. ☐ Presents	7. ☐ Special Edition	11. ☐ Other _____
3. ☐ American Romance	8. ☐ Intimate Moments	
4. ☐ Temptation	9. ☐ Desire	
5. ☐ Superromance		

2. Number of romance paperbacks you purchase new in an average month:

12.1 ☐ 1 to 4   .2 ☐ 5 to 10   .3 ☐ 11 to 15   .4 ☐ 16+

3. Do you currently buy romance
series through direct mail?   13.1 ☐ yes   .2 ☐ no

If yes, please indicate series: _____
                                                    (14,15)   (16,17)

4. Date of birth: ____ / ____ / ____
                      (Month)   (Day)   (Year)
                       18,19   20,21   22,23

5. Please print:
Name: _____
Address: _____
City: _____ State: _____ Zip: _____
Telephone No. (optional): (____) ____

MAIL TO: Attention: Romance Reader Panel
         Consumer Opinion Center
         P.O. Box 1395
         Buffalo, NY 14240-9961

Office Use Only   TDK

PASSPORT TO ROMANCE
SWEEPSTAKES RULES

1. **HOW TO ENTER:** To enter, you must be the age of majority and complete the official entry form, or print your name, address, telephone number and age on a plain piece of paper and mail to: Passport to Romance, P.O. Box 9056, Buffalo, NY 14269-9056. No mechanically reproduced entries accepted.

2. All entries must be received by the CONTEST CLOSING DATE, DECEMBER 31, 1990 TO BE ELIGIBLE.

3. **THE PRIZES:** There will be ten (10) Grand Prizes awarded, each consisting of a choice of a trip for two people from the following list:
   i) London, England (approximate retail value $5,050 U.S.)
   ii) England, Wales and Scotland (approximate retail value $6,400 U.S.)
   iii) Carribean Cruise (approximate retail value $7,300 U.S.)
   iv) Hawaii (approximate retail value $9,550 U.S.)
   v) Greek Island Cruise in the Mediterranean (approximate retail value $12,250 U.S.)
   vi) France (approximate retail value $7,300 U.S.)

4. Any winner may choose to receive any trip or a cash alternative prize of $5,000.00 U.S. in lieu of the trip.

5. **GENERAL RULES:** Odds of winning depend on number of entries received.

6. A random draw will be made by Nielsen Promotion Services, an independent judging organization, on January 29, 1991, in Buffalo, NY, at 11:30 a.m. from all eligible entries received on or before the Contest Closing Date.

7. Any Canadian entrants who are selected must correctly answer a time-limited, mathematical skill-testing question in order to win.

8. Full contest rules may be obtained by sending a stamped, self-addressed envelope to: "Passport to Romance Rules Request", P.O. Box 9998, Saint John, New Brunswick, Canada E2L 4N4.

9. Quebec residents may submit any litigation respecting the conduct and awarding of a prize in this contest to the Régie des loteries et courses du Québec.

10. Payment of taxes other than air and hotel taxes is the sole responsibility of the winner.

11. Void where prohibited by law.

COUPON BOOKLET OFFER TERMS

To receive your Free travel-savings coupon booklets, complete the mail-in Offer Certificate on the preceeding page, including the necessary number of proofs-of-purchase, and mail to: Passport to Romance, P.O. Box 9057, Buffalo, NY 14269-9057. The coupon booklets include savings on travel-related products such as car rentals, hotels, cruises, flowers and restaurants. Some restrictions apply. The offer is available in the United States and Canada. Requests must be postmarked by January 25, 1991. Only proofs-of-purchase from specially marked "Passport to Romance" Harlequin® or Silhouette® books will be accepted. The offer certificate must accompany your request and may not be reproduced in any manner. Offer void where prohibited or restricted by law. LIMIT FOUR COUPON BOOKLETS PER NAME, FAMILY, GROUP, ORGANIZATION OR ADDRESS. Please allow up to 8 weeks after receipt of order for shipment. Enter quickly as quantities are limited. Unfulfilled mail-in offer requests will receive free Harlequin® or Silhouette® books (not previously available in retail stores), in quantities equal to the number of proofs-of-purchase required for Levels One to Four, as applicable.

OFFICIAL SWEEPSTAKES
ENTRY FORM

Complete and return this Entry Form immediately—the more Entry Forms you submit, the better your chances of winning!
- Entry Forms must be received by **December 31, 1990**
- A random draw will take place on **January 29, 1991**   3-HT-2-SW
- Trip must be taken by **December 31, 1991**

YES, I want to win a PASSPORT TO ROMANCE vacation for two! I understand the prize includes round-trip air fare, accommodation and a daily spending allowance

Name_____

Address_____

City_____ State_____ Zip_____

Telephone Number_____ Age_____

Return entries to: **PASSPORT TO ROMANCE**, P.O. Box 9056, Buffalo, NY 14269-9056

COUPON BOOKLET/OFFER CERTIFICATE

Item	LEVEL ONE Booklet 1	LEVEL TWO Booklet 1 & 2	LEVEL THREE Booklet 1, 2 & 3	LEVEL FOUR Booklet 1, 2, 3 & 4
Booklet 1 = $100+	$100+	$100+	$100+	$100+
Booklet 2 = $200+		$200+	$200+	$200+
Booklet 3 = $300+			$300+	$300+
Booklet 4 = $400+	____	____	____	$400+
Approximate Total Value of Savings	$100+	$300+	$600+	$1,000+
# of Proofs of Purchase Required	4	6	12	18
Check One	____	____	____	____

Name_____

Address_____

City_____ State_____ Zip_____

Return Offer Certificates to: **PASSPORT TO ROMANCE**, P.O. Box 9057 Buffalo, NY 14269-9057

Requests must be postmarked by **January 25, 1991**

- ✂ - - - - - -

 ONE PROOF OF PURCHASE   3-HT-2

To collect your free coupon booklet you must include the necessary number of proofs-of-purchase with a properly completed Offer Certificate

See previous page for details